COVER OF DARKNESS

GREGORY DELAURENTIS

This is a work of fiction. The events, situations and locations described here are imaginary. The settings and characters are fictitious and not intended to represent specific places or living persons.

COVER OF DARKNESS

To Mom and Dad

DIVIDED INVESTIGATION

The pool area was wide and reflected the sun on this hot summer day. It was edged with white marble so polished that it looked like pearl. Deck chairs lined the sides of the long pool, which was two lengths more than Olympic-sized. Outside the deck area was the carpeted lawn of the vast backyard, dappled with sun.

Hugh Osterman walked along the side of the pool wearing a heavy terry cloth robe and sandals. In his right hand, he held a martini glass. He ran his left hand through his sandy sun-streaked hair as he looked over his shoulder at the man following him.

"What's going on? I don't get it," Osterman said, stopping at the end of the pool where the flotation chairs were kept.

"They said no," the man replied. Considering the backdrop, he was incongruously dressed in a dark suit and tie.

"They said no... just like that?"

Osterman sat his drink down on the marble surface, and pushed a flotation chair into the deep end of the pool, sending it out and away. Then he peeled off the robe and dove smoothly into the water, emerging next to the floating chair.

"You go back and tell them that we aren't pleased," Osterman said sternly, pulling himself up and into the seat of the chair. "You tell them that Hugh Osterman wants to know what's holding things up—what the problem is."

The suit just stood at the edge of the pool, opening his jacket against the heat of the day. Osterman paddled to the side, and reached out and retrieved his martini glass. "I take it you have nothing to say about this?" he persisted, despite the other man's silence.

The suit shook his head.

"Well, what are you waiting for?" Osterman said as he tipped the glass up to his lips. Suddenly, the bottom of the stem shattered. Osterman gurgled as he dropped the glass, blood bubbling from his mouth, an open tear in his neck. He jolted upright in the chair as the suit closed the distance between them, his Colt .38 Super still trained on its victim, its silencer smoldering.

Osterman slowly sat back as the suit pumped more rounds into Osterman's bare, well-defined chest—the hot shells of his pistol ejecting out and striking the surface of the water, settling to the bottom. His life ended as his body tumbled from the floating chair, his blood a widening crimson slick roughly in the area where his body slipped through.

The suit popped his clip, slipped in a new one, and headed for the sprawling house.

A long winding driveway led up to the gated entrance of the Osterman estate. Pine and spruce trees dotted the grounds, which were well-tended and spacious. Now this broad peaceful area was marred by a melee of police cars and white and blue vans parked in front of the house, the entryway door blocked by yellow crime scene tape.

Police captain Sam Jefferies ducked under the tape and entered into a large atrium. His salt and pepper hair atop his head was curly, with a beard and moustache stubble ringing his face. His face was long and his eyes were tired and red from getting poor sleep. Immediately to his right was a clique of CSI lab people with bowed heads, standing over a body on the floor: the corpse was a male dressed in a shirt, black tie and slacks, a pool of blood under his head. He lay in a crumpled heap, apparently dying in mid-motion, as if he'd just turned away from the gun blast that felled him.

Jefferies joined the group. As his eyes took in the murder scene, he was approached by Lieutenant Franklin Clinton, a tall black man in his forties who couldn't help but look fashionable in a gray pinstripe suit. A thin moustache lined his upper lip, his short afro curly, his hairline receding. "Three stiffs," he announced to Jefferies as he stopped just short of the body.

Jefferies nodded grimly and asked, "Butler, housekeeper and owner?"

"Butler, *squeeze* and owner," Clinton replied.

"Where's the squeeze?"

"This way," Clinton said as he led Jefferies around a wide spiral staircase, the floor under their feet polished black marble. Large windows with open blinds shed bright sunlight inside the palatial home.

They entered a dining area where a grisly scene awaited them: the white tablecloth that covered the near end of the large dining room table was streaked with radiating sprays of blood, bone, and brain matter, while on the far end it was gathered into the fists of a young woman leaning face down across it. A dime-sized portion of the back of her skull was missing, and what could be seen of her forehead was a bloody pulp-rimmed exit wound. She was sprawled across the table naked, the lower half of her body hanging off the side. Her two-piece pink bikini was on the floor at her feet.

More CSI people were milling about, a forensic photographer firing off photographs. They passed by the two detectives, forcing them back.

Jefferies leaned over to Clinton and in low tones said, "Rape?"

"Could be. Who knows yet?" Clinton shrugged.

"This is kinda messy, even for a pro," Jefferies remarked.

"Doesn't look like a professional hit to me. This looks more recreational."

"What… the whole shebang?"

"No, just this. Osterman is outside in his pool," Clinton said flatly, as he shepherded Jefferies toward the glass doors of the dining room which opened onto a wide patio with an imposing brick barbeque pit off to the right. To the left was a sundeck with deck chairs, tables, umbrellas, and a crushed marble walkway that wound downward around colorful landscaped flowerbeds to the pool area below.

"Who was this guy, anyway?" Jefferies asked.

"Hugh Osterman made his fortune on Wall Street as a bond trader, where he still worked. He also ran a club in the city called the Midnight," Clinton said as they came alongside the pool.

"Obviously he's not hurting for money."

"Well, he was hurting a few hours ago when several slugs were pumped into his chest."

"From what?"

Clinton kept walking until he stood over the body now rigid on the marble edge of the pool, covered over with a white sheet from head to toe. "A thirty-eight, nice and neat."

"Any outstanding leads?"

"Neighbors heard shit," Clinton said. "A silencer must have been used. We believe that the butler got it when he opened the door, which means that the killer was known."

"He had to be known to get through the driveway gate." Jefferies used his hand to shield his eyes from the sunlight, as the two men walked toward the marbled path to the back of the mansion. "What else?"

"From the position of the shells in the pool, the killer was on the far end with Osterman, who didn't have a clue that it was his last day on earth. After the killer was finished here, he went into the house and found the girl. He might have raped her on the table at gunpoint."

The two men entered the mansion and this time headed off to the den, which was broad and roomy and comfortably furnished. At this point, Clinton reached into his jacket, produced a pad and flipped it open. "The female victim is Pamela Walker. We found her purse and wallet upstairs in the master bedroom."

Jefferies strode over to a leather-clad loveseat and pressed it several times to test its softness. Then he turned around, plopped himself down and leaned back with a groan. "What are we doing with this case, Frank?"

Clinton frowned, "Captain?"

"This will go the usual route, right?"

"It should. He's just a Wall Street wonk that got whacked. Probably over something stupid."

Jefferies stretched his arms out across the top of the loveseat, and gave a tired sigh. "Damn, they make these things comfortable, don't they?"

Clinton merely hunched his shoulders in reply.

"Run with it, see what you get," Jefferies said. "But I want a copy of the report. I have another idea."

"Idea?"

"Yeah. Another one."

Clinton nodded and walked off, leaving Jefferies alone to glance around the den.

DOUBLE DOWN

Kevin awoke on the couch, stretching his arms and his legs, while his head remained firmly on the cushions.

"About time you woke up," David said.

Kevin rolled over and narrowed his eyes at his roommate sitting on the easy chair across from him. "S'up?" he groaned, slipping his legs off the couch.

"Why don't you ever lift a finger to clean up this dump?" David looked around. "I'm tired of being the one to do it all the time."

"I clean," Kevin looked around, frowning. "Was I drinking? I feel as if I have a hangover."

"Not that I know of." David sat up in the chair and leaned over his knees as he spoke. "Were you?"

"Not that I know of." Kevin stood up wearing nothing but his boxer shorts and stepped into the bathroom. He called out, "What time is it?"

"Late, motherfucker—get a watch."

Kevin went to the mirror, looked at himself, ran water in the basin, washed his face—and then looked at himself again.

"Don't worry, you can't wash it off, white boy," he heard David say behind him, as he headed toward the kitchen. "Who's cooking dinner?"

Kevin followed his roommate and said, "Throw something in the microwave."

"We've got nothing to throw into the microwave, dude."

"Then, let's have a beer."

David snapped his fingers. "There you go! Now you're talking." He made it to the refrigerator in two steps, opened the door and grabbed two cans. "Read my mind, buddy."

He tossed the can, and Kevin caught it. "By the way, we got a call from Sam earlier."

"Jefferies? What did he want?"

David popped the top on his can and took a swallow. Then, silence. For someone who loved beer as much as he did, he was slim and muscular, his shoulders and rippled arms protruding from the sleeves of his T-shirt. David's skin was dark, his face a group of handsome lines and smoky bedroom eyes. The hair was cut to stubble on his head, so short that it only colored his scalp, making him appear nearly bald.

Kevin frowned. "What did he want, Dave?"

David burped, still in no hurry to speak. "He has a case for you," he said finally.

"Oh, really?"

"Yeah, he said to keep your ass sharp."

Kevin opened his beer and said, "You tell him I don't do pro bono work anymore?"

"I told him I don't want to talk to him anymore. I'm through with his bullshit."

"What'd he say?"

"He said to put you on the phone. I told him you were asleep."

"That's cool. Another case. It's been a long time." Kevin turned and strode off to the living room.

"Remember the last one," David said, following him. "You almost got your scrawny white ass killed."

Kevin scowled, as he seated himself at the office desk. The living room of their apartment also doubled as an office for them; on one wall was a desk with laptop and printer, on another wall was a bookshelf filled with books. A flat-screen television was mounted to one wall and in the center of the room was a loveseat, couch, easy chair and low coffee table.

"You just love to bring that up, don't you? You just will not let that go, will you?"

"Well, I did have to come to your rescue," David said, pointing at him with the can of beer in his hand. "You were screwed, buddy."

"'You were screwed, buddy,'" Kevin mimicked sourly. He turned on the laptop on the desk and donned his glasses, which were on the desk beside it. "You just called the cops."

"What the fuck?" David took quick offense, his mouth and eyes wide. "I plugged a motherfucker, and fist-fucked the other, while you were having your ass handed to you." He paused for a sip of beer. "*Then*, I called the heat and Jefferies came with the cavalry."

"Sure, sure," Kevin leaned closer to the computer screen to give David a sure sign that he was no longer listening.

"What are you doing? Checking email?"

Kevin did not reply.

"Fuck it, then." David strolled back to his easy chair and kicked up his feet on the coffee table.

"I'm checking for Margaret's email."

"How are you and that chickenhead doing?"

"Why do you keep calling her a chickenhead, Dave?"

"Because she doesn't like me... Kev."

Kevin sighed.

"So—how are you and the chickenhead doin'?"

"We're fine," Kevin said as he quickly scanned his emails. After finding nothing, he closed the top of the laptop angrily, and turned in the chair to face his companion. "So, what are you going to do today? Sit here and harass me?"

"Harass you?" David stood, rested his can of beer on the coffee table in front of the chair, and strode across the room to the coat closet. "Harass you? I'm going down to the precinct to see Jefferies."

"I thought you said you weren't speaking to him anymore."

David produced a coat from the closet and slipped it on. He reached up to the shelf atop the coatrack and came away with his holstered .38 snub-nosed revolver. He checked to see if it was loaded, and then holstered it.

"Do you need to take that?" Kevin asked with obvious concern, his normally clean shaven and carefree countenance now frowning. The flowing hair, always groomed, still looked neat even after waking from the couch. Kevin looked like a prep student, with his glasses and youthful features.

"That's the problem with you, Kev," David pointed out. "You don't believe in firearms. That's what's going to get you killed because, believe it or not, there are bad guys out there that don't share your religion."

"A good detective uses his head, not his hands."

"It's hard to use your head when it's a blood splatter." David clipped the holster to his belt and covered it up neatly with his coat. "Anything you want me to tell Jefferies for you?"

"Tell him that you're taking the case this time, not me."

"Yeah, sure."

David opened the door and came face to face with Margaret, who was standing on the other side poised to knock. She jumped back, startled, when the door opened. "David!"

David looked over his shoulder at Kevin. "Kev, it's your chickenhead, who's been spying on us through the door."

"I wasn't spying," Margaret protested as she stepped around David to enter the room.

Margaret was a tall lean brunette who was surprisingly attractive and appealing with her relatively plain features and large, light blue eyes. Her hair spilled over her shoulders in straight lines, her lips pink, small and thin.

"I'll see you later, Kev," David said as he slipped out the door, closing and locking it behind him.

Margaret removed her handbag, dropping it onto the couch, and then took off her coat and draped it across the back. "How can you live here with him, Kevin?" she asked. She approached and gave him a quick peck on the lips.

"He's been my partner for years."

"So what?" She looked around, surveying the room. "Well, at least he cleans up. You're a damn slob, Kevin."

Kevin stood up, took her by the wrist and pulled her along behind him saying, "Come on, let's go to bed."

"Oh, no," she countered as she broke his wrist-hold on her. "You've got to take a shower, find a decent suit and go with me to my mother's house."

"What?"

"You promised me, Kevin."

"C'mon. You've got to be kidding me."

"You promised."

"But I've got this case that David and I are working on."

"Just a second ago you wanted to go have sex."

Kevin thought about that for a moment. "It would only take a second."

"That's appealing. You are impossible, Kevin," Margaret huffed; then she paused, and struck a pose with her hand on her hip. "Well?"

"Well, what?"

"Are you going to take that shower?"

"Baby," Kevin gestured to the door. "I've got a case. I've been called in to see Jefferies."

"You're dealing with Jefferies again?"

"Yeah."

"Didn't you get all beat up on your last case? If it wasn't for David—"

"Not this shit again." Kevin stomped around in a circle like a petulant child.

"Kevin, I'm warning you. If you don't take a shower and come with me to my mother's, I'm walking out that door and I'm not returning."

"Baby, I love you, but I got a case," Kevin pleaded, holding his hands out for her. He closed in on her gradually, and she backed away, furious.

Finally, Margaret turned around, snatched up her coat and purse, and stormed out of the apartment, slamming the door behind her.

"Shit," Kevin said to himself, scratching the back of his head. "But she'll be back. She always comes back."

David entered Jefferies' office at One Police Plaza. He spotted the captain standing across the room, his lean frame in silhouette against the large window behind him as he gazed at the scene below. He turned around to greet David when he heard him come in. Jefferies was an older man, but at fifty-six he still got about like a man twenty years younger. At times, he carried himself like David, shoulders squared, ex-military man, and at other times he carried the exhausted deportment of a police captain overburdened with cases.

But Jefferies was at this for a long time. All his life all he knew was the police force. His father was a cop and his father before that when there were mobsters.

Jefferies grew to a mature man as an officer, then detective. And then he met Kevin, a raw recruit in the police academy.

Jefferies' office was Spartan and clean with a long bureau against the wall on the right made of the same dark wood as the wide desk back near the wide window across from the door. Atop the bureau was a mini-coffee maker and stacks of folders. Next to the door a black leather couch lined the wall on the left and in front of the desk sat two straight-backed chairs.

"Hey," Jefferies said, going from tired to alert. "It's *you*."

"Yeah, Jefferies."

Jefferies paused and then looked puzzled. "David?"

"Yeah, Jefferies. Who does it look like?"

"David. I thought you said you were through with me."

"So, I lied." David strolled into the office and sat down in one of the two straight-backed chairs directly facing Jefferies' desk. "You got a case for me?"

"For the two of you." Jefferies strode over to his mahogany bureau and picked up a fat folder filled with papers and photos. "How's Kevin?"

"He's alright." David shifted in his seat, trying to get comfortable. "He said he's out of this one."

"I'm sure," Jefferies said as he reached over the desk to hand the folder to David. "He's always out of it until he sees the paperwork."

"Yeah, he's good with paperwork." David took the folder, and began flipping through it. "He's not worth a damn in the—" he stopped talking as he pointed at a photo. "Was she getting fucked?"

"Yeah, forensics pulled ten cc's of semen out of her."

"Shit, he blew her head off."

"Damn near."

David frowned. "But why go and rape her? Or was it rape?"

"Vaginal tearing, lack of lubrication, that kind of shit."

"I see."

"Pamela Walker, twenty-five years old."

"What was the scenario? Why her?"

"The prime target was apparently Hugh Osterman, a forty-eight-year-old white male."

David flipped through more papers. "Westchester?"

"Yeah. Police up there think they need more firepower on this. They asked for a detective squad from One Police Plaza to come and take a look at the scene. It seems that Osterman was a big wig up there. Or knew some big wigs up there."

"I'd like to take a look at the crime scene."

"You got it, Dave. How do you plan to get up there?"

David smirked. "I'll get the 'fraidy cat to drive me up."

"Yeah, take him with you." Jefferies rested his elbow on the desktop and rubbed his eyes with a thumb and forefinger. "Take the file—let Kevin look it over too—and see what you can do. I'll make arrangements for you to see the crime scene."

The door to the office opened and in walked Franklin Clinton. He stopped short when he noticed David in the room. "Oh… it's you."

"S'up, brother?" David nodded.

Clinton frowned. He turned to Jefferies. "This guy again, Captain?"

"This guy again, Frank."

"Well, Sam, I can see I'm not wanted here." David closed the folder and stood up to leave.

"I'll have some officers waiting for you at the crime scene," Jefferies said, sitting back in his chair. It creaked under his weight.

As David walked past Clinton, he nodded in his direction and said, "Take care, bro'."

"Fuck you, man."

Without making any reply, David walked out of the room and closed the door softly behind him. The instant he heard it close, Clinton turned on Jefferies. "Sam, you can't be serious. That guy's nuts!"

"What are you talking about? He's fine. He's a damn good detective."

"He's been off the force since his 'little accident.' "

"I've been giving him work. He's on a department pension; he's not in need of money. He's a sharp officer and a good cop. He shouldn't be wasted."

"Is this why you wanted another copy of the file?"

"That's what he carried out of here." Jefferies stood up from his chair and walked over to the window, contemplating the view. "He— and probably Kevin too—will be on this case like white on rice."

"That's what I'm afraid of. Didn't Kevin almost get killed last time?"

Jefferies nodded. "He was lucky. However, that goes with the territory. And this will be difficult territory too if the rap sheet on Osterman's squeeze is any indicator."

HEADACHE

Photographs and police reports were scattered across the kitchen table. Kevin tipped back on two legs of a kitchen chair, a beer in one hand, a forensics report in the other.

"Toxicology reports tons of cocaine in her bloodstream," he said.

"So, she was a snow bunny." That said, David stood up from his chair and retrieved a slice of pizza from the box where it rested on the countertop.

"Yeah, a serious one. She had near toxic levels," Kevin said as he leafed through pages. "I doubt if she even knew her head was almost taken off."

"Most people don't." David smirked, and he took a bite.

Kevin looked up from the report. "What does her rap sheet look like?"

"Messy, very messy," David said as he chewed his food, leaning back against the counter. "Bad girl. Busted for carrying, mule-ing, prostitution, assaulting a police officer. All the usual dumb shit."

"Yep—sounds like a bad girl." Kevin closed the report and tossed it on the tabletop. He lifted the can of suds to his mouth and drank deeply before speaking. "You going up there?"

"And you're driving."

"I figured that. What about Osterman? He was a big civic leader in the town. You think that's why he was whacked?"

"Could be. Maybe he was putting the political nut crush on some freak in town politics."

"But what was he doing with a snow bunny?"

"Fucking her most likely, Kev."

"You know what I mean. He's a fine upstanding figure in the community, no?"

"I would suppose so."

"Then why be caught literally dead, with a known lowlife like Pamela Walker?"

"Maybe her little pale ass was irresistible. Seven out of ten hit men think so."

Suddenly, Margaret entered the kitchen from the direction of Kevin's bedroom and said, "Hit men think what?"

"Nothing," Kevin said, shifting his position to upright in the kitchen chair.

Margaret stepped over to get a closer look at the documents on the table. She paged through some of the reports quickly, before she noticed the full-color photographs of the bloodied corpses. She closed her eyes and walked away, a hand to her mouth. "Ugggh, how can you guys eat with those pictures around?"

"You get used to it," David said, taking another bite of pizza.

Evidently recovered from the gory sight of the photos, Margaret went to the box of pizza, reached in and took a slice for herself. "The corner pizzeria?"

David nodded, standing next to her, still chewing.

"How was your mother's?" Kevin asked.

"She was very disappointed in you, Kevin." Margaret turned around, and still standing, rested her back against the counter. "I told her you were sick."

"She believe you?"

"Of course, she believed me. Why would she think I would lie?"

"Because you did," David chuckled.

"Shut the fuck up, David."

"Temper, temper."

"Alright you two," Kevin interjected. "We're working a case here, Em."

"Yeah? I can't hear?"

"How 'bout we show you more forensic photos?" David said.

Margaret sighed deeply, before turning toward him. "If you don't leave me alone, David Allerton, I swear to God I'm going to give you such a slap that you'll feel it for days."

"Ooooh," David cowered. "I'm so scared."

Kevin ignored them while he rifled through the papers on the table until he found the report he was looking for, and thumbed through it. "Osterman is survived by an ex and three children."

"And—?" David asked.

"Maybe it was a revenge killing. His wife hired a hit man to clean her husband's clock and polish off the squeeze."

"Polish off the squeeze?" Margaret asked.

"Could be. Want to go and check her out?" David said, addressing himself exclusively to Kevin.

"Not so fast. She could be in mourning."

"Fuck that. Not if she killed him."

"Why would you think it was her?" Margaret asked.

"If he was shacking up with a girl half her age," Kevin replied. "His business partner is also a suspect."

"What business were they in?" David asked, as he finished off the last slice of pizza and casually tossed the crust back into the box.

"Import/export," Kevin said.

"Company is being embezzled by Osterman. His partner finds out and has him wacked. End of story."

"That sounds reasonable," Margaret remarked.

"We just need to get info on the company. Maybe a quarterly report if they're publicly traded," Kevin said, as he continued to peruse the pages. David approached the kitchen table and went through some of the papers, producing a stapled sheaf of papers. "Alright, the two detectives from One Police Plaza that are working the case are Ferryman and Reynolds. Know them?"

Kevin nodded. "Ferryman is pretty good. Reynolds is an old hack waiting to retire. He'll try to skate through this case—do a very superficial investigation."

"So, Sherlock Holmes, where do we go first?" David asked. "All of this mental masturbation is making me tired."

"Let's start at the filthiest part—Pamela Walker's family."

"Ooooh, that's good, Kevin." David nodded.

"Is that the dead girl?" Margaret asked.

The silver Ford Taurus turned slowly onto the tree-lined street in Queens and pulled to a stop directly across from the home of Pamela Walker. Kevin shifted the car into park and kicked on the hazards.

"This is it—1133 Thirteenth Avenue," Kevin said, staring out the driver's side window at the simple two-story house across the street.

"Good. Look, you go in and do your thing," David said. "I'm going to sit back here and take a nap."

"Sure," Kevin said as he undid his seatbelt and opened the driver's side door. "What if I get in a jam?"

"You know," David said with a smile. "Just give me your patented rape scream and I'll be there in a flash."

"Very funny," Kevin said as he slipped out of the car and slammed the door shut behind him. He crossed the street, pushing his glasses up the bridge of his nose, straightening his tie and shirt collar, and buttoning up his jacket.

A waist-high chain-link fence bordered the property all the way around. Kevin opened the gate and headed for the front door. As soon as he placed his foot on the short flight of steps leading up to it, there was a growl, deep and guttural, close by. Kevin froze—his finger just inches away from the bell. Looking down and around, he saw a large pit bull loping from the side of the house. But the dog didn't see Kevin as it raced past him and began barking at some kids on the other side of the fence who were running down the street. While the animal was distracted, Kevin decided to ring the bell. At the sound, as if on cue, the dog immediately turned away from the fence and charged to the bottom of the steps, barking angrily at Kevin, who retreated onto the top landing, and placed his back to the door.

"Down, Satan!" A woman's voice called from the side of the house. "Go on, get out of here! Git!"

The dog stopped barking as soon as the woman emerged from the side of the house, and shooed him away. Satan trotted off to the other side of the house, but kept an eye on Kevin—who exhaled deeply—as it departed.

"Can I help you, mister?" The woman came to the foot of the steps. She was matronly, heavyset and in her fifties, with wisps of gray in her hair and large pendulous breasts.

"Hello ma'am, I'm Kevin Whitehouse." Kevin reached into his jacket pocket and produced his ID, handing it over. "Private detective. I'm investigating the murder of Ms. Pamela Walker."

She took the wallet, opened it, checked the face and then closed it, handing it back. "I've already talked to the cops."

"Would you mind giving me just a moment of your time?" Kevin asked.

The woman paused to think about it, and reluctantly agreed.

Kevin stashed his ID and then withdrew a small Integrated Chip recorder. "Do you mind if I record you? It's better than writing down what you say on paper."

"I guess so."

Kevin took a moment to turn on the recorder. "Who are you, ma'am?"

"Mrs. Estelle Walker—Pamela's mother," she replied.

"Sorry for your loss, Mrs. Walker. And her father?"

"He's dead," she said flatly. "Been that way for several years now."

"Sorry to hear that."

"I'm not. The sonofabitch was no good to begin with. Left me with two kids to raise on my own. He died of the big disease with the little name. Good for him."

Kevin frowned. "Big disease?"

"AIDS."

"Oh, drug user?"

"Shot heroin."

"And your daughter?"

"What about her?"

"What was your relationship with her?"

"I was her mother."

Kevin shook his head. "Were you close, I mean?"

"Hell, no. That child was a hellcat since she turned sixteen. She was boy crazy, you know. And they would hop her up on all these drugs and do things to her—" she shook her head at the recollection, "—she was just all messed up."

"Did she live with you?"

"On and off, depending on her boyfriend at the time. When one threw her ass out, another would take her in, the penal system would lock her up, or she'd come home."

Kevin nodded. "When was the last time you saw her?"

"About a month ago. She dropped by for some money, saying that she was in the 'big leagues' now. Whatever that meant. So I asked her, why the fuck do you need money from me then?"

"Did she say?"

"No, but it was for dope most likely. It was always for dope."

"Did you give it to her?"

"Yeah, I gave her a hundred dollars. She was my daughter, you know."

"Yes, I know. Do you know who her close associates were?"

"A red-headed girl named Karen was her running buddy. They were like two peas in a fucking pod. She lives somewhere in Brooklyn."

"Is that the only information you can give me about her?"

"Oh, no. Her name is Karen Francis, and her phone number is—" Mrs. Walker rattled off the number from memory.

"They must have been close, or you wouldn't have her number memorized."

"I've got a good memory."

"Well, thank you for the information, Mrs. Walker." Kevin reached into his jacket pocket and produced one of his business cards, handing it over to her. "If you remember anything else, anything to help us find her killer, please give me a call."

Mrs. Walker cautiously took the card. "Is that it?"

"That's all, Mrs. Walker. Quick and painless."

Kevin opened the car door, slipped back into the driver's seat and slammed the door shut, waking David. He yawned and blinked, and then asked, "How'd it go?"

"I almost got ate by a dog, not that you care." He held out the IC recorder and pressed play. Mrs. Walker's voice came through loud and clear, chanting out Karen Francis' phone number. "Call division, give them the number and tell them to check the reverse lookup for an address."

David sighed, reached into his jacket, and withdrew his smartphone.

David walked up the white marble steps of the Osterman residence with Kevin trailing. A black and white cruiser pulled up behind their Ford Taurus, and one of the local cops got out and strode up the path toward them as they stood at the top of the stairs.

"You David Allerton?" the officer asked, his two-way squawking that an 'unidentified' was approaching the Osterman home.

"Yeah," David replied, getting out his ID.

The officer shook his head, ignoring the ID when it was held out to him. "Your captain called it in." He walked over to the front door and pulled away the sealing tape that read police do not cross. Then he unlocked the door and swung it open. "We'll be out here waiting to lock up when you're ready to leave."

"Thanks," Kevin said.

David stopped just inside the threshold. He looked around and then up at a huge crystal chandelier in the center of the ceiling. It gleamed with the slanting sunlight from the set of high windows facing it.

"Why," Kevin began, "do you always insist on visiting the crime scene? You can get all of this stuff in the reports."

"Photographs don't give you the mean distances or the feel of the surroundings like being there, Kevin. That's why you suck in the field."

"The 'field' can be a dangerous place."

David looked down at the large bloodstain still on the floor, where the body of the butler had lain just inside the door. "It was for him," he said as he pointed down at the dried puddle with his hand fashioned into a gun. "He was plugged first, right away."

"What gives you that impression?" Kevin asked sarcastically.

"First at the door, of course," David continued, evidently not catching the inflection. "The killer must have had a silencer. Plus, he probably slid the gun back inside his jacket to block the smell of cordite."

The two walked through the atrium. The expansive kitchen area encompassed a large wide space, awash with the light emanating from the floor-to-ceiling glass doors that led to the backyard. In the center of the kitchen was an island consisting of a stovetop, sink, and work surface. On it stood a silver decanter, an ice bucket, long-stemmed martini glasses, and a bottle of tonic water.

"The killer probably ran into Hugh Osterman here—" David pointed to the paraphernalia on the counter "— making a drink. According to the report, he had a busted martini glass on the bottom of the pool. They talked. Osterman led him out of the house." David paused as he opened one of the sliding glass doors and stepped outside into the backyard. He looked around and found the walk leading down to a grove of trees. Kevin followed silently.

"They talked, walked, came down here." David traced a path straight to the outsized pool. "Osterman never saw it coming. He walked to his flotation chair and caught seven shells."

"Six," Kevin corrected.

"Six. The killer didn't have time to reload."

"Not for one bullet," Kevin added.

"Six shells all the fuck over."

"One in the neck, the rest to the central mass. A rubout for sure."

"Yeah," David agreed. "This appears to be a professional hit: silencer, accuracy, number of dead all over. Someone was very clear about what he was doing."

Kevin nodded.

"Osterman knew his killer. It wasn't someone new to the house. His business partner?"

"What was his business partner? Special forces or something? I don't think so," Kevin replied. "This was obviously someone who had been up here before though, at a party or something."

"Well, the killer went back up the path," David said as he started walking the way they came. "Probably reloaded on the way up and ran into Pamela, maybe sunning herself on one of the deck chairs."

"He was probably hopped up on adrenalin, nerves all afire. She kicked his libido into overdrive. He showed her the gun and took her into the dining area." Kevin was pointing out the areas as he walked, entering the house and heading for the dining room.

"Which he had to know of beforehand."

"Right," Kevin said. "He draped her over the table, raped her and shot her in the head."

"Now that's very *un*professional." David went up to the blood-stained tablecloth. "He could have just shot her as she sat in the lounge chair."

"If that's where he caught up with her." Kevin looked around the room. "This is a pretty big place."

"That's why a silencer is so good here. Hard to hear it."

"Are we done?"

"Why? Don't you want to pay a visit to Karen Francis?"

"No, I've got to get home. Margaret and I are going out to dinner."

"You do that," David said, walking into the den and glancing around at the rich antique furniture and heavy red drapes. "I'll get the black and white to take me to the nearest bus stop back to the city."

"Why? I'll drop you off."

"You go to your chickenhead. I'll go interview this Karen Francis."

"Have it your way," Kevin said as he headed for the front door. "Take care—see you tonight." He trotted down the stairs to the circular driveway where the Ford and the squad car waited. One of the two officers in the vehicle waved him away. He waved back. Starting the engine, he drove back to the city, leaving David behind.

THREE'S A CROWD

The brownstones lined both sides of the Brooklyn street, with sparse trees offering little shade. Kids played in and around the parked cars, and a dog jumped about happy to be among them. As David walked down the street, his eyes scanned his surroundings carefully. There were two old women chatting as they sat on chairs at the top of a stoop. A group of teenage boys leaned against a parked car. Finally, he came to the address he was seeking; it was a nondescript brownstone, exactly like the rest, but with no sign of life anywhere around it. Even the windows looked blank and empty.

David went through the gate and climbed the stone steps to the front door. He pressed the button for apartment three. The buzzer rang, there was a click, and David opened the door. He climbed more flights of stairs, and on reaching the second landing, he saw a red-headed woman leaning over the railing above, watching him coming up.

"You're not Daniel."

"No, I'm not," David replied. "I'm David Allerton—a private investigator." He reached into his jacket and produced his ID, holding it up in her direction as he reached the third floor.

Karen shrugged it off. "So?"

"May I ask you a few questions?" David jammed his ID back into his pocket and brought out his IC voice recorder.

"What for?"

"Did you hear about Pamela Walker?"

"Yeah, I heard. I've already talked to the police."

David noticed that she was attractive, young, probably in her twen-
ties. She had a lean body and a pale face, with light freckles across the
bridge of her nose. "Like I said, I'm a private investigator."

"Yeah," she said flatly, "I heard about Pam. Tough break. She had
it good, though."

"What do you mean by that?"

"Are you recording me?"

"Yeah, I hope you don't mind. It's better than writing things down."

"I see. Well, she got her sugar daddy, didn't she?"

"You're talking about Hugh Osterman?"

"Whoever."

"How did you and Pamela meet?"

Karen shifted her position to rest her body against the banister of
the stairs. "We were club girls. We met at a club called the Arcadium.
She liked to party, I liked to party. We just got along with each other."

"You two were snow bunnies?"

"What do you mean?"

"You know what I mean. Cokeheads—for your time."

"We followed the parties, if that's what you mean."

"That's what I mean. So, she moved in with you?"

Karen sighed wearily, "Is this going to be much longer?"

"No, not long. Did she move in with you?"

"Off and on… whenever her boyfriends kicked her out."

"And Osterman was her latest 'boyfriend'?"

"Who, mister?"

"Her sugar daddy."

"Yeah."

"Did she leave any personal effects?"

"Yeah, she left some of her shit."

"Can I see it?"

"No. The cops took them away in a box. They took everything."

"Cops. Were their names Ferryman and Reynolds?"

"Yeah, something like that. Older guys, you know? Is that it?"

"Just one more question. When was the last time you saw Pamela alive?"

"Last week. She came here for some of her clothes and paid me some money for last month's rent. That's when she told me all about her sugar daddy upstate."

"All good news?"

"All good news."

David turned off the recorder. "Thank you, Ms. Francis."

Margaret was watching Kevin as she leaned against the kitchen counter, running her fingers through her long brunette hair. "The minute we get back, you're in the kitchen with the reports."

Kevin tossed a stack of documents on the tabletop. "I told you, Em. We're working a case."

"I know that. But did you have to take a side trip to One Police Plaza to pick up your silly transcript?"

"Everything on paper and on the table as soon as possible, that's the deal. I just got the interview with Mrs. Walker transcribed so—there it goes." Kevin's cell phone chirped. He pulled it out of his jacket to answer it.

"S'up, boss," David said.

"What's up, Dave?"

"Where are you?"

"Home."

"I just finished the interview with Ms. Francis. She wasn't much help. She's just a snow bunny."

"Dead end, huh?"

"Pretty much so."

"Where are you off to now?"

"I'll be taking the subway home after I drop off the recording of the interview at the One Police Plaza typing pool for transcription."

"Alright. Tomorrow is another day."

"Later."

"Later."

Margaret lurched from where she was standing. "Well, I'll leave you to your case," she said haughtily.

Kevin stood over the cluttered table, as if studying the reports from a distance. "See ya."

Kevin awoke in his bed, a tangle of sheets, pillows without pillowcases and soiled clothing. He slid off the edge to his feet. Wearing only boxers on his scrawny body, he shambled into the hallway on his way to the bathroom where he took a long, luxurious leak, yawning all the while. Afterward, he strolled across the living room and into the kitchen where he hovered over the table. He found David's IC recorder on top of the stack of papers, and picked it up. Pressing play, he listened to the conversation between David and Karen Francis. David had no doubt given the device to the people in the typing pool earlier to make a copy of the digital file for transcription.

"You're up on this already?" David said from behind him, entering the kitchen dressed in pajamas.

"Yeah," Kevin said, still listening to the recording and scratching his head through his tangled mane of dark hair. "Did you ask her about whether she knew other friends of Pamela's?"

"No, I didn't think she would be helpful. She was really closed mouth; you know, like one-word answers." David opened the refrigerator and took out a carton of orange juice. "I'm going to follow her Thursday night."

"Not Friday night?"

"No, young people today sometimes go out on Thursdays. It doesn't matter. I'll catch her going out. She's a party girl, she'll be out more often than not." David took a glass from the cupboard and filled it with juice. "What do we have on the agenda today?"

"I'm going out with, Margaret…"

"*Again?*"

"Hold on, hold on," Kevin admonished. "We're going out shopping. But if I do that for *her*, she has to come with me to the ME's office so I can get the reports on the corpses."

"Sound's good. You want company?"

"Make it a threesome? You've got to be kidding. You two will be at each other's throats."

"Don't pin that on me, partner." David took a swallow of juice before continuing. "She's the one with the problem."

"I'm not blaming anyone, and she doesn't have a problem, Dave."

David placed the carton on the countertop, and turned to lean up against it. He pointed to Kevin with the hand that held the glass. "You like that creepy fuck, don't you?"

"Who? The medical examiner?"

"Yeah. That creepy Asian vampire chick."

"Susan is not a creepy vampire," Kevin protested.

"You let Margaret find you snuggling up with that chick and she'll bust a cap in your ass."

"I'm not snuggling up to anyone, my friend. And I would appreciate it if you wouldn't talk about things like that."

"Why not?"

"Just in case Margaret ever hears you talking that shit."

"What shit?" Margaret asked as she strolled into the kitchen, went directly over to the table and started flipping the photographs over onto their faces.

"That he's really in love with the assistant ME in the medical examiner's office," David said.

Kevin made a face at him behind Margaret's back.

Margaret sighed heavily. "David, you are so full of shit. That's the reason why Kevin said you talk shit. Who even listens to you?"

"Kevin," David said with a wide grin on his face.

Margaret turned her back on him to face Kevin. "Are you going to get dressed?"

"Yeah," Kevin said, as he left the kitchen.

Margaret continued to stand with her back to David while he finished his orange juice, turning the glass up, over his face.

"David, you and I don't have to love each other, that much we agree—"

"—I don't like to talk to the back of people's heads, Em," he interrupted.

She turned around, scowling at him. "I've asked you not to call me Em."

"Sorry. Margaret."

"Can we just get along for the sake of Kevin? Is that even possible?"

"I don't know, Em. We just happen to be two people who don't get along. And we don't have to just to make things easy on Kevin. You think he's going to move in with you, and that will be the end of me. And I think he's going to find another ho, and that'll be the end of you. We're both just playing for time."

"Right now, you two are on a case together. Just do me a favor and watch over my man like you did before."

"Well, that's one thing we agree on, sista."

***

Kevin and Margaret entered the lobby of the medical examiner's office, a large room with comfortable sofas. Overlooking busy First Avenue was a large bay window on the right. On the left, police officers stood behind a long, high guard desk. Margaret was holding shopping bags in both hands, while Kevin had one. They stopped in the center of the lobby where Margaret said, reluctantly, "I don't want to go in with you."

"You never want to go in with me."

"I don't like dead bodies. I'll wait here for you. Don't take long."

They walked over to a couch. Kevin left his shopping bag at her feet as she sat down and repeated, "Don't take long."

"I'll be right back."

When Kevin walked over to the guard desk, the officer recognized him immediately. "Whitehouse. Nice to see you, buddy."

"Sands—how are you?"

The black officer cracked a broad smile, came from around the desk and held out a hand, which Kevin shook. He looked slim in his uniform and tie, a thin moustache beneath a wide nose and sharp eyes. "I'm doing good. You know what life is like here with Rawlings." He motioned with his chin to the officer at the door standing guard.

"Fuck you, Sands," Rawlings said, cracking a smile. He was slightly heavier than Sands, his face clean shaven, his cheeks on the chubby side. Rawlings looked like a suburbanite who would be standing over a grill on the weekends with a steak fork in one hand and a beer in the other.

"How the fuck are you doing, Whitehouse?" Sands continued.

"Fine, Sands."

"I mean *really*. How have you been, boss, since the accident?"

"I'm doing good. Really good."

"Damn, that's nice to hear, buddy." Sands slapped Kevin on the shoulder several times. "You going in?"

"Yeah. Is Ito in?"

"Susan? Yeah, she's up there."

"Alright, I need a pass."

Kevin walked toward Susan Ito's office slowly—peeking in the doorway—and found it empty. As he turned away, she suddenly appeared and walked past him into her office.

"Kevin Whitehouse," she said.

"Susan." Kevin replied, as he entered and closed the door behind him.

She walked over to her desk carrying a cup of coffee and set it down. A diminutive long-haired Asian, she looked very attractive even in a long white lab coat.

She turned to face Kevin and crossed her arms across her ample breasts. "Come here for the report?" she asked.

"And a walkthrough, if you don't mind."

"Why would I mind, Kevin? I live for this shit." Susan snatched up her coffee and said, "Come on."

They exited her office and traveled down several corridors to reach the morgue. They entered through a set of double doors into a large open space filled with steel tables upon which bodies lay, covered with white sheets. All about them were rolling tables covered with instruments. The lighting was dim since most of the overhead high-hat lamps were off, while against the wall a few light boxes glowed only to illuminate x-rays.

Another set of double doors led them to the refrigerated drawers. Susan walked up to one column and pulled on a handle waist-high from the floor. It slid open smoothly, revealing a body covered with a sheet. With the same hand, she snatched back the sheet, exposing the blue-white face of Hugh Osterman. There was a hole the size of a pencil eraser in his neck where the Adam's apple would have been.

"Here's your cadaver," Susan said. "He's pretty much standard other than the fact he was peppered with thirty-eight caliber bullets."

"Nothing unusual?"

Susan took a sip of her coffee. "He had a large amount of cocaine in his bloodstream."

"Just like the girl," Kevin said.

"Just like the girl."

"That's it?"

"As far as I can tell, Kevin, he was shot to death. The one through the heart caused him to bleed out the fastest. His stomach contents reveal that he had a healthy breakfast before he was killed, and toxicology also found a substantial amount of alcohol in his system."

"Nothing that stands out?"

Susan shook her head while looking intently at Kevin from the other side of the drawer. "Are you still with what's-her-name?"

"Margaret."

"Yeah, her. The mystery girl."

"She's no mystery. She's right in the lobby, if you care to meet her."

"And why would I want to do that?"

"Yeah, I'm with her, Susan."

"So we go out on a few dates, pal around a little, and that's it? I was that piss poor of a partner?"

"No. It's just that Margaret is a better match to my personality. She's like my right arm."

Susan smirked. "You have your accident and then you meet this complete stranger on the street, and now you two are inseparable."

"It's been a year, Susan—"

"I know, and I should move on. I'm seeing another guy now, but you and I had so much potential, so much chemistry."

Kevin reached down and threw the sheet back over Osterman's cold dead face. "Yes, we did, Susan."

"And you feel nothing for me now?"

"Susan. It's been a year."

Susan slammed the drawer shut and walked to the double doors. "Come with me, I'll give you the report."

Kevin followed her back into the examination room. She walked to a central table covered with folders, thumbed through a stack, and produced one. "Hugh Osterman. Cold and dead and nothing outstanding. Completely underwhelming." She crossed the distance to Kevin and slapped the folder against his chest, pinning it there. "Completely underwhelming."

"Thanks," Kevin reached for the folder, but found that Susan still had it pinned against his chest.

"Kevin, why do you insist on coming here to pick up these reports? I file them with Jefferies in a timely manner and you can get them straight from him. Like Pamela Walker's, when I finished hers. This is completely unnecessary—unless you're coming here to see me."

As Kevin mulled over her statement, he took a step back so that Susan released her grip and let him have the folder. "I want a walk-through, like I said."

"I've told you before, every time you come here you just make it harder for us to disconnect."

"Us or you, Susan?"

"You keep coming back here, Kevin."

He grew silent again.

"I'm through," she said as she turned and walked out, leaving Kevin standing alone in the meager light of the examination room.

***

David had followed Karen Francis into the city. It was about ten o'clock at night. He pulled up several car lengths behind her taxi as it pulled to the curb. She slipped out of the cab and onto the sidewalk. She was dressed in a blouse with a plunging neckline, a miniskirt, and high heels. After waiting for the cab to pull out, Karen crossed the street to the club, its entrance lit with neon and flashing lights. A crowd of people milled around in front, some smoking, others just waiting to get in. She approached the bouncer standing at the door, showed her ID, and immediately gained entry.

David rolled up his car windows, turned off the engine, and stepped out into the night. He waited for a car to pass ahead of him before crossing the street and approaching the bouncer. He held out his hand, stopping David before he could pass by.

"Fire code, buddy. We're at capacity," he said.

"What about the woman that just walked in?" David asked, removing the pair of aviator shades he wore to be less recognizable to Karen should she happen to glance his way.

"Fire code, buddy, you'll have to get on line."

David reached into his pocket and flashed his badge.

"Oh, sorry about that, bud," the bouncer said, stepping aside.

After first replacing his shades, David entered the club and negotiated his way through the crowd. The place was packed with young people, drinking, talking and dancing, while hip-hop music blasted from the loudspeakers. He scanned the dance area —lit with multicolored pulsating strobe lights—and saw nothing but unfamiliar faces and shadows. After finally working his way over to the crowded bar, he ordered a gin and tonic. When he scanned the length of the bar, David saw Karen Francis talking with a group of women, laughing loudly and striking poses. He noticed that they weren't ordering drinks.

David paid for his own, then moved from the bar to the wall. From there he observed Karen as a group of tipsy, well-dressed businessmen converged on her small clique. One tall blond man kept leaning over and whispering in Karen's ear; and while cupping his hand surreptitiously, he passed something small to her, after which she immediately headed to the bathroom.

David kept his eye on the blond male. After Karen's little group broke up—each pairing off in a different direction with the suits—one unlucky girl was left standing at the bar alone with the blond male. She leaned over toward the bartender and ordered a drink.

Karen returned shortly and handed something back to the blond guy. When the two of them headed out, David left his drink on a nearby table, and followed them. Once on the sidewalk, they walked unsteadily down the block and turned into a parking lot, closed for the night, blocked off from traffic by a long padlocked chain hung across the entrance. The couple then staggered into a dark corner of the lot where the street lights could not reach. David took out his mini-telescope from his pocket to watch them. The suit unzipped his fly to uncover his erection, and Karen dropped to her knees to swallow it.

David, putting away his telescope, crossed the street silently to lean against a nearby wall where he could keep an eye out for them, unobserved. In less than fifteen minutes the couple emerged from the lot, and the blond guy walked to the corner to hail a taxi. Karen headed back in the direction of the club.

David came up behind the suit, grabbed him by his collar and pulled him backward, catching him off guard. He staggered as David spun him around and drove him face forward into a phone kiosk.

"*What the fuck*!" the suit exclaimed angrily.

David shoved his badge into the phone kiosk in front of the guy's face. "Go ahead, talk bad. Weren't you the one just getting a blowjob in a public area?"

"Awwww, shit man—" The suit sighed.

"Keep talking bad."

The guy sighed, then relaxed. David released him and allowed him to turn around to face him. "What am I going to get, a summons?"

"Lewd and lascivious behavior, and public indecency? I don't think so, buddy." David replaced his ID and removed his cell phone from his pocket, opened it, pressed a button and put it up against his ear. "District, send a van to pick up a tough guy—"

"*Oh, please, mister!*"

"Hold on—" David looked at the suit. "What?"

"Please, officer. This is the first time this has ever happened to me—I swear. I just met this girl in a bar down the street and she invited me into the lot over there." He pointed in that direction with his chin.

David closed the cell phone and slipped it into his jacket. Then he reached over to pat down the suit's chest, and felt something in the inside breast pocket. He reached into the jacket and pulled free a vial of cocaine.

"Oh, this is getting better and better. Is this what you gave her inside of the club?" David asked.

"You—you were watching?"

"Now, you want to stop lying?"

"That's not mine, officer—"

"Shut up." David put the vial into his jacket. "Who was that you were with?"

"Her name is Karen," the guy said dejectedly. "She runs with a pack of bitches who'll do anything for a little coke."

"Snow bunny?"

"That's about right."

"Do you know Pamela Walker?"

"Pam?"

"Pamela Walker?"

"I don't know her last name. I know a Pam, though. Tall girl, dark hair, pretty hot looking, nice bod, has a husky voice?"

"That could be her, yes."

"She's a snow bunny too."

"I know that. Tell me something that I don't know."

"I don't know what else to tell you, sir."

"Do you know a Hugh Osterman?"

The suit swallowed. "*Mr.* Osterman?"

"You know him from work?"

"Yeah, he is—was—the CEO of the company I work for."

"Osterman-MacDonald?"

"Yes, the investment firm. They own Club Midnight."

"They own this club?"

"And several others around the city."

"Have you hung around with Mr. Osterman?"

"No—never!"

David looked at the suit for a moment. "You going home now?"

"Yes, sir."

"Say several Hail Mary's, and don't jerk off."

The suit stood speechless.

David backed away until he put some distance between himself and the suit, then turned and walked off. He smiled to himself at the suit's ignorance. A cop wouldn't call into Division on a cell phone, but rather a radio.

Returning to the club, David headed to the corner of the bar, found the unlucky girl still there, but no Karen. He waited a few beats to be sure that Karen hadn't just stepped away momentarily, and then approached Ms. Unlucky. She turned to him, cracked a wan smile, and then returned to her drink. David leaned against the bar, staring into her face. "S'up?"

"Hello," she replied.

"What's up with you?"

"What do you mean?"

"All your friends hook up and leave you behind? What's up with that?"

"That's just the way it happens sometimes."

"Well, I guess it worked out for me then."

"How so?"

"Want another drink?"

She looked at her glass, turned it up and drained it. Placing it on the bar, she returned her dark sultry eyes to David. "Dirty martini."

David beckoned to the bartender and ordered drinks.

"So what happened to you, mister? Date stood you up?" Unlucky asked.

"David Allerton," he said as he held out his hand.

"Mary Olman." She shook his hand.

The woman was young and had a flawless complexion, unblemished by a single mole or freckle. Fair, with rosy cheeks, she had a broad, toothy grin that lit up her entire face.

"No—no date. Just here by myself, looking around for someone nice to talk to." David said.

The bartender returned with their drinks. Mary took hers as she asked, "Is that a fact?"

"That's a fact." David took a big belt out of his gin and tonic.

"David," Mary said. "Do you have any coke?"

David smirked, reached into his jacket and produced the vial, flashing it quickly in front of her face before replacing it in his pocket.

Mary's face suddenly lit up like Christmas.

"You want to party?" Mary asked cautiously, despite being excited by the idea of the coke so close at hand.

"Here, why don't you get started?" David again fished the vial out of his jacket and handed it to her. Taking it quickly, Mary took off for the bathroom. David finished his drink and waited for her to return. When she did, she thanked him and gave him back the vial. She was noticeably more relaxed and upbeat than before.

"Now, can I ask you a few questions?"

"What's that, Dave?"

"Do you know Pamela Walker?"

"Pam? Yeah. She's dead." Her tone was cold and matter-of-fact.

"Do you know how she died?"

Mary blinked—she was high already. "She met this old man here—one of the owners of the club—and he started wining, dining and sixty-nining her. I read in the paper they were killed together in his crib up in Westchester."

"That's right. Can you tell me anything about them? Anything that she told you about herself and Mr. Osterman?"

"She said he was kinky," Mary replied as she drained her drink once more.

"In what way?"

"He liked fucking her in public."

"Really, now? What's so kinky about that?"

"I wouldn't do it."

"I'm not too sure about that, Mary."

She held up her glass. "Can I have another?"

"Sure, order away. I'm running a tab."

NO CLOSER TO THE TRUTH

David woke up with the back of Mary's hand in his face. He pushed her over gently and got up from the bed naked. He grabbed his boxers from the floor and his robe from the back of a chair, put them on and then headed for the bathroom. When done urinating, he entered the kitchen to find Kevin face down on the table, asleep. David massaged his neck to wake him up, and after a time, Kevin sat up slowly.

"What are you doing sleeping out here?" David asked, going to the freezer compartment of the refrigerator and pulling out a box of frozen waffles.

"The chick that you brought home last night is a screamer."

"Screamer?"

"Every time you gave her the meat, she yelped like a small dog."

David laughed. "She did, didn't she? I was too busy smacking that twenty-five-year-old ass."

"You get a kick out of the shit you do, don't you, Dave? You just have no bottom, do you?"

David pulled out a frozen waffle from the box and began eating it. "Bottoms are for losers."

"Well, did you learn anything?"

"Osterman owns a club in midtown called Club Midnight. That's about it."

"That's not good. I thought you were going to come up with something hot."

David shook his head, then reached into the box and produced another waffle.

"Aren't you going to put those in the toaster?" Kevin asked.

"What for?"

Kevin shook his head.

"What about the body? You and Ito fuck?" David asked.

Kevin smirked, "No, no one did anything. I came back with the report. It's pretty straightforward. He was shot to death."

"Let's consider the fact that the shooter was a contract killer. We may never make the leap to find him." David pointed at Kevin with the half-eaten waffle in his hand.

"The only good thing is that he was known to the household. That's better than a fingerprint."

David nodded, burped. "Did Osterman and Walker's cell phone records come through yet?"

Kevin stood up from the chair, rifled through the growing mess and lifted two stacks of stapled papers. "Right here. Delivered yesterday."

David set down the waffle box and took the records. Flipping through them, he commented: "About a hundred. That rules out straightforward police work."

"What would that be?"

"Knock on every door on the list."

"If we split it up—"

"We split up and you'll get your dumb ass killed before you finish the first twenty. Margaret will murder me if anything like that happened to you. Go through this by frequency and give me the numbers in the city most often called. I'll go knocking on the doors."

"*David!*" Mary called out, her voice booming from the bedroom. "I'm in here naked!"

David handed back the phone logs to Kevin. "Work calls."

About an hour later, dressed in his robe again, David went straight to the kitchen table and searched for the phone records, which were nowhere in sight. "Shit, Kevin must have taken them," he mumbled to himself.

"You know," Mary called out. "Your friend is kind of sloppy! His room is a mess."

"Yeah, I know," David yelled back as he flipped through the papers again, but found nothing new.

Mary came up behind him dressed in panties and a bra. She embraced him from behind, wrapping her arms around his waist. "What's your plan for today?" she asked.

"I'm driving you home and then I have a little work to do."

She looked over his shoulder and then down at the paperwork on the table. Her eyes caught on one of the forensic photos and she came around David to get a better look at it. As she lifted it up, she said, "Good God, that's fugly." Then she blinked. *"Oh, my God!"* she exclaimed, recognizing the blank face of the victim. "It's Pam!"

David reached over, and with two fingers quickly plucked the photograph from her hands and tossed it aside. "Strictly private detective stuff."

Mary looked at the table, then back at David. "Did last night happen just because you're investigating Pam's death?"

"Look, don't bother playing wounded with me," David replied. "You're here because you were following the coke and I was supplying. Simple as that. I didn't give you any other assurances."

"Can a cop deal coke like that?" she asked, stepping back from him.

"I told you, I'm not a cop. I'm a private detective."

"And who are you working for?"

David walked to the refrigerator and produced a small block of cheese. He looked at it, noticed that someone had taken a bite out of it, and returned it to the fridge. "That's my business, little girl. Now get dressed and I'll take your little snow bunny ass home."

"David—"

"What?" David closed the refrigerator.

"Do you know who did that to her?"

"Not a clue."

Mary hesitated for a moment before she said, "You should ask Two Smooth."

"Too who?"

"Two Smooth, like the number two." She held up two fingers. "He runs around with a pretty tough entourage."

" 'Pretty tough' meaning?"

"Scary tough." Mary brought a hand to her throat, massaging it.

"Why? Why do you bring him up?"

"No reason, really," she said, biting her lower lip and looking worried and pale—the forensic photo had obviously shaken her.

"What did you little ass ponies get yourselves into?"

"A few of us did some parties for him."

"*Did* parties?"

"You know, show up at parties to provide some eye candy."

David leaned against the refrigerator and said flatly, "You did some prostitution for coke or crack."

"Well, I wouldn't call it prostitution."

"Did you fuck some stranger?"

"Yes."

"Prostitution."

"Women have sex with strangers all the time," she said with a scowl.

"Women *are* prostitutes."

"Very funny." She smirked at him before she left the room.

David left his post and followed her. "Tell me more about you fucking for Two Smooth."

"I wasn't having sex *for* Two Smooth," she said, stopping in the middle of the living room and turning to face him. "I met a very nice gentleman there who was a lot of fun—and he wanted to do fun things."

"Awwww, cut the shit, Mary! I don't have time for this. I'm interested in a murderer that likes to fuck, and blow pretty young girls' heads off their shoulders. Now can you help me or what?"

She made a sour face as she went over to the couch to look for her skirt. "Well, at one of the parties this guy slapped one of the girls around and these two gorillas came in and dragged him out. The last time we heard about him the guy was in the hospital."

"Being gorillas doesn't make them killers. You've got to do better than that."

Mary finally found her skirt on the floor, and put it on. "They were scary, David, really scary. And I saw a gun on one of them."

"You wouldn't happen to know if these goons were off-duty cops, would you?"

"No."

David thought about it. Since he had no other leads, this one was as good as any. "Where can I find this Two Smooth?"

"I really don't know. He comes to the Midnight and his entourage picks up girls for the evening. Then we all go to an expensive hotel— you know, the kind with the adjoining rooms?"

David nodded. "Which one?"

"The Marriott Marquis on Broadway," Mary said as she finally found her blouse, which had been draped over the back of a chair.

"That's good enough," he said.

"You can find him?"

"I was a skip tracer, baby," David said as he headed for the bedroom to get dressed. "I can find anyone."

David drove Mary home to her apartment in Brooklyn, which she shared with another young woman. He stayed for a coffee and Danish and bullshitted with Mary for a while, finding her entertaining and charming. She was obviously protective of her roommate, Cheryl, because she kept trying to draw the shy pretty blonde with the sleek page-boy haircut into the conversation.

Mary had a nervous habit of constantly running her fingers through her long black hair like a self-conscious high school kid might do. David found this trait endearing and wondered if she inspired something of a paternal instinct in him.

Soon it was time for him to leave, and as he said his goodbyes, he told Mary that he would be too busy to see her that night.

When David got back to his car, he headed for midtown and struggled through the afternoon traffic on Broadway before he found a parking lot with a space available for his Ford. He walked quickly up the crowded street to the Marriott, and went straight to the escalators to avoid the security desk, situated just before the bank of elevators. He rode up to the huge lobby area, and approached the concierge.

To the sunny-faced woman who greeted him, he said, "Do you know anything about a certain celebrity who was here with a large party, and rented out several rooms all on the same floor?"

"I'm sorry, but we can't give out that kind of information," she said.

David showed her his Private Investigator's badge. She glanced at it, and then turned around to speak with an officious-looking young man in uniform, gesturing to David as she spoke—with both of them casting nervous glances at him.

"Hello, officer," the young man said as he stepped over to David.

"What would you like to know?"

"I need the address of a certain 'Two Smooth' who stayed here last month."

The young man looked down at a computer screen behind the desk, his fingers tapping away on the keyboard. "No, no one here by the name 'Two Smooth' in the last three months, sir."

"How about someone renting multiple rooms on one floor?"

The keys clicked again. "Three organizations and two people."

"Skip the organizations. Who are the two people?"

"A Mr. Winston Strawn, and a Mr. T. S. Williams."

"That's him," David said, trying to peer over the counter at the monitor. "That's him. T. S. Williams."

"He has a Park Slope, Brooklyn address listed here." The young man found a pencil and paper nearby and began scribbling.

"Great—thanks for the help."

Handing over the piece of paper, he said, "It was my pleasure, sir, and thank you for choosing the Marriott Marquis."

"I don't see why *you* have to go and do this, Kevin," Margaret said from the passenger seat of the car. Kevin turned a corner, then slowed the car down while he stared out at a row of expensive brownstones off Central Park. "Someone needs to talk to him."

"But that's what David is for. He's the one who's good in the field."

"Where do you get that from?" Kevin asked as he double-parked in front of one of the brownstones and turned on his hazard lights.

"From the last time you went off on your own, and had your ass handed to you." Margaret looked at him with an expression of utter seriousness.

"No one handed my ass to me," Kevin snarled. "You and David are always bringing that shit up. I had everything perfectly under control until David stirred the pot and caused it to overheat."

"With you getting burned."

"Look," Kevin gestured at the brownstone as he spoke, "just look at the neighborhood we're in. How could anything dangerous happen here?"

"I don't know. Why take the chance?"

"Because, like I said—someone has got to speak to him. Now you stay here and stand guard."

Margaret nodded nervously, dug through her bag and produced her cell phone, waving it at him as she said, "I'm staying on the cell phone. If you don't come back in fifteen minutes, I'm calling Jefferies to bring the cops."

"I'm sure he will too," Kevin reassured her. "Fifteen minutes."

"Fifteen."

Kevin leaned over to give her a peck on the cheek, but Margaret jerked her cheek away. He opened the car door and stepped out, closing it behind him. It was dark, and the air was unseasonably cool for late August. He studied the brownstone from the outside first, counting all of the lit windows. Most of the nearby floor-to-ceiling windows were bright. Kevin walked around his Ford and climbed the stairs to the front door, pausing for a minute before ringing the bell.

After a brief wait, the door opened and a young blonde woman stood before him. Her blue eyes were only half-open yet visibly bloodshot. She was clad in a tight black dress, and kept one hand on the doorknob while holding a martini in a long-stemmed glass in the other.

"Can I help you?" she slurred.

Kevin held up his badge. "Kevin Whitehouse, ma'am, private detective."

She leaned forward, squinting at the badge, frowning, and then cursed under her breath. "I can't read that shit." She continued to frown. "What do you want?"

"Can I come in?"

At that, she flung the door open, staggering back unsteadily on her feet. "Be my guest," she said as she turned and sauntered off through a high-ceilinged atrium furnished with blood red carpeting and elaborate antique chairs, tables and gilt-frame mirrors.

Kevin closed the door behind him softly, and followed her on a winding path through the house. The house was much larger on the inside than it had appeared from the outside. Kevin trailed behind her as she entered a kitchen, another enormous space, decorated in stark white. There was nothing silver but the knives.

"What it this, heaven?" Kevin said, half-joking.

"It is now." The woman crossed to an island in the center of the kitchen. A bottle of vodka sat on the countertop with four rows of white powder. She took a hundred dollar bill, rolled it between her two hands, stuck it up her nose and snorted two lines. "Shit, that feels so good," she sighed afterward.

"You don't have the slightest worry about doing that in front of a cop?" Kevin asked.

"You said you were a private dick," she replied, straightening up.

"Is Mr. MacDonald in?"

"Are you a cop?"

"If I were one, do you think you'd still be standing there now?"

She wiped her nose with her hand. "No, I guess not."

"Now, is Mr. MacDonald in?"

"Who? Stew?"

"Yes, Stewart," Kevin replied testily. "I'd like to talk to him about his business partner."

"Who? Hugh?" She chuckled.

"Yes, Mr. Osterman."

She made a face as she said, "He ain't here. He's out doing business with his other business partner."

"His *other* business partner? Don't you know that Hugh Osterman was murdered?"

She took a casual sip from her martini glass. "I know."

"Well, can you tell me where… Stew went? I would like to talk to him."

"Probably running around with Two Smooth and his bunch."

"Who?"

"Two Smooth. Know him?"

"No. Can you can fill me in?"

She looked down at her high heel shoes, then back up at Kevin. "These are Manolo Blahniks. I have a bunch of them. Stew bought them. Do you know what that means?"

Kevin shook his head. "No."

"I don't fuck him over."

"Look, I'm not asking you to snitch on your meal ticket. I need to talk to him or he might end up just like his partner. And I know you know what happened to his partner's lady friend."

She thought about it. "What's the chance of that shit happening to us?"

"Who knows, maybe if I had a chance to talk to Stew, he would be able to tell."

"If something went wrong it came from Two Smooth's side of the fence, that's for certain," she said as she pointed at Kevin with her glass.

"Now, who is this Two Smooth?" Kevin asked pointedly, taking a step towards her.

"He runs a stable of women for parties and shit like that. We did a side gig—well, I used to do it, as a side gig."

"Whose? Yours and Macdonald's?"

"*No*—myself and the girls."

"The girls at the club?"

"Yep." She wobbled on her feet as she spoke.

"Where are they? Have any idea?"

"Somewhere in Brooklyn. I've never gone there myself." She waved her hand, dismissively.

"Do you know what kind of *business* they're in?"

She shook her head, and added illogically, "Look, mister, I don't know who you are, but you're no cop, so all of these questions aren't enforced by the law…"

"Like I told you, I'm here to help, not to harm—believe it or not," Kevin said.

She scrunched up her face, finished her martini, and then turned her bloodshot eyes in Kevin's general direction. "Two Smooth deals in everything. He's a form of entertainment provider. He works for Huey and Stewie. The three of them were pretty tight."

"I can imagine. Do you have any idea where I can find this guy, Two Smooth?"

"Nope." She again snatched up the hundred-dollar bill, leaned over the counter and did another line. "I've only seen him at the Midnight."

"The club."

"Yeah, that's right."

Kevin glanced at his watch and noticed that his fifteen minutes were up. "Look, if you can give me any more information on Two Smooth, could you please contact me?" He produced a business card from his pocket and laid it on the counter next to her remaining line of coke. "Also, let MacDonald know that I'd like to speak to him as soon as possible. I can be reached at the number that's there on the card."

"Sure," she said agreeably as she smiled at him drunkenly. Then she reached out and picked up the card—squinting her eyes as she tried to read it. "What does this shit say?"

Kevin shook his head. "You need to lay off the doping and drinking.

Drugs and alcohol don't mix."

"Thanks, pop."

David sat in the dark in his Ford, parked in Englewood Cliffs, New Jersey, on a two-lane road in the woods, high up in the rolling hills. This was definitely a 'keep the fuck off' road. He had stationed himself across from a pair of tall, wrought-iron gates that broke a space through a tall rock wall.

He had cut a U-turn and headed back down the street a few yards, busted another U-ey, and pointed the vehicle at the gates. That was three hours ago. He had turned off the ignition so he wouldn't kill the battery. Soon the cigarettes came out of the glove compartment. He never really liked stakeouts, although he knew how to handle them. Like a corpse, he could wait anywhere, on anyone, for hours on end. This was something that Kevin was bad at. Kevin was better with the interview, with talking to someone who didn't want to talk. He was a good interrogator. David would rather just stab the person behind their kneecap to get their attention.

Suddenly, the gates swung open slowly. A black limousine lurched out of the driveway and onto the road, its headlights cutting through the dark ahead. It turned left and rolled past David—there was no doubt the occupants were checking out his car. After passing the Ford, the limo sped up and headed down the road. David threw his cigarette butt out of the window, turned on his headlights, shifted into drive and made another U-turn. His car slipped smoothly behind the vehicle at a respectable distance.

"Ten to one there's another 'brother' in that limo," David muttered to himself.

***

When they returned to the apartment, Kevin was still thinking about his interview with the doped-up blonde. "Shit, dead end," was how he finally summed it up to Margaret.

"When are you going to get a real couch, that's what I want to know," Margaret complained once she had settled down on the lumpy threadbare couch.

"This Two Smooth is the best lead we've got. If he, MacDonald and Osterman were so intertwined, then we have a definite connection here."

"You're sure *you* want to be the one to tangle with this Two Smooth? Why don't you leave him to David? He sounds like a gangster—the tattooed, gun-toting type." Margaret brushed away crumbs and other debris from the couch cushion next to her, before reclining across it. "You don't even carry a gun."

"Do you want me to?"

"Oh God, no," she exclaimed as she held out an imploring hand. "I really don't. I take that back. You'll just put yourself into dangerous situations like David does—"

"You sound as if you'd rather David risk *his* life. Almost as if it holds less value."

"Less value to me." She bit her lower lip before she added, "Kevin, you are my lover, not my lover's friend. There is a marked difference."

"Well, we're going to have to find this Two Smooth anyway—"

There was a knock on the door.

"Who could that be?" Kevin asked.

Margaret sat up, and then stood up.

Kevin crossed the living room and looked through the peephole. "Oh," he mumbled before unlocking the door and holding it open. Two suited men strolled in, looking around the room with a mixture of caution and interest.

"Good evening, Whitehouse," said the one nearest Kevin. George Ferryman was tall and lean with gray streaks in his hair. His face was long and distinguished, clean with blue eyes and a pearly smile. His suit was wrinkled and his tie was slack and cocked to one side.

"Police talk. I'll be in the kitchen," Margaret said tiredly, almost to herself. She waved a hand at Kevin's guests disappearing into the kitchen.

"Whitehouse," the other detective, Arnie Reynolds said, sounding a bit cheerier. His suit looked new, his tie was cutting edge, and his aviator glasses were perched atop his crew-cut hair. He seemed half the age with twice the energy of his counterpart. Reynolds made himself at home in Kevin's apartment, making a beeline for the bookshelves where he started examining several of the books, until he held one up. "I've got this one," he remarked.

Ferryman sighed. "You're shadowing our investigation?" he asked.

"Yeah."

"Are you getting anywhere with this? These people don't like talking to the police."

"Yeah—well, right now we're hung up on a suspect," Kevin replied.

"Who?"

"Some thug named 'Two Smooth.' He appears to be a chum of Osterman and MacDonald. They were said to be inseparable. Do you know of him?"

"No, not in our area," Ferryman said as he reached into his jacket, withdrew his pad and pen and started scribbling. "I'll check around with our informants."

"Thanks."

"What does the kitchen table look like?" Ferryman said with a laugh.

"You know, nothing new. What about you guys? Did you find anything that stands out?"

Reynolds slipped another book from the shelf, opening it and flipping through the pages. "That girl, Walker, was part of a group of about ten snow bunnies. They were a pretty rough crowd of women."

"Rough, huh?"

"He means licentious," Ferryman explained. "Pretty severe whores."

"Expensive, I would presume."

"Not really. That's what Reynolds means when he said, 'rough crowd.' They're not all that discriminating about who they do what with," Whitehouse explained.

"I guess when times are tough you have to put aside the caviar dreams and champagne wishes," Kevin mused.

"I guess."

"Hey!" Reynolds again held up a book. "You mind if I borrow this one?"

Kevin shrugged his shoulders. "Take it. They're David's books."

"You talk to Mrs. Walker?" Ferryman asked, stashing away his pad.

"Estelle Walker? Pamela's mother?" Kevin asked. "Yeah."

"What did you get from her?"

"Guys, take a seat. Let me get you our transcript." Kevin gestured to the beaten sofa.

"That's alright," Ferryman gave a slight nod. "We'll stand."

Reynolds plopped down into a nearby easy chair, where he opened the book in his hands and flipped through it once more.

Kevin left the room to get the transcript of his interview with Pamela's mother.

"What do they want?" Margaret hissed from the sink where she stood washing dishes.

"Share information," Kevin said as he rifled through the papers. "They want a peek at our personal transcripts of interviews that we've done."

"They can't get those at One Police Plaza?"

"No, these are ours. We get them transcribed at the secretarial pool, but we get the only copies. They belong to us."

"Find anything out from them?"

"Nothing new just yet."

Kevin found the document he was after, and returned to the living room where he announced to his colleagues that he would make a copy for them. He crossed to his desk, laid the papers on his printer pickup tray and pressed copy, and the copies slid out through the other side of the device.

"She didn't really give up any information," Kevin said as he straightened out the papers.

"You guys are so good at using technology to your advantage," Ferryman observed. Police work seemed to be getting to him. His stance was slightly slouched and his face was careworn—he almost looked dead on his feet.

"Why? Is something the matter with that?" Kevin said as he handed over the copy of the transcript.

"We're still scribbling notes on pads at the department."

"Well, David and I have a unique relationship when it comes to our investigations. We're seldom together, so we have to find other ways of communicating. Like keeping the newest findings in a central location, which for us is the kitchen table."

"Transcripts and stuff."

"That's just about it. And then we have it handy too, for others, if we feel the need."

"I see." Ferryman's expression grew somber. "How are you doing, Kevin?"

"Fine, why?"

"Everyone worries about you, you know?—since you dropped out of the force."

"Yeah, I know. Crossed over the thin blue line. But I'm fine."

"Tired? Headaches? Stuff like that?"

"Naaah."

"Good then. Seen your therapist?"

"Not in a while now."

"You should keep in touch with him. Not that I'm in your fucking business, you know." Ferryman chuckled, gave Kevin a punch to the shoulder.

"I know."

"Well, thanks for this." Ferryman held up the transcript, now rolled into a tube. "I'll get back to you as soon as we find anything on this Two Smooth character."

"Alright. Great."

Ferryman turned to Reynolds. "Come on, Arnie. It's time to go."

Reynolds pushed himself out of the old beat-up sofa and joined Ferryman at the door. "Have a good day," Reynolds said brightly, following Ferryman out.

"Take care," Kevin said as he closed the door, put his back against it and exhaled deeply. He noticed that Margaret had suddenly appeared in the center of the room, her arms crossed over her chest.

"Now that's the best idea you've had throughout this entire investigation," she said.

"What's that?"

"Leaving it to the cops to interview the suspects—and not trying to do it all yourself."

Kevin stepped away from the door and approached the bookshelves. "You know how I hate for Ferryman to one-up us."

"Who cares about that shit, Kevin," she said testily. "You'd better watch your ass, or it could be handed to you."

Kevin rearranged the books on the shelf so that David wouldn't find any space between them. "Don't worry about that so much. I'll be fine."

"You're right. I worry about you too much. I have my own life to live."

Kevin turned around to face her. "Now, what is that supposed to mean?"

"It means that I'm heading home. I'll talk to you later," she answered as she crossed the living room to the front door.

"Yeah."

"Try not to get yourself killed before I get home."

"Very funny."

"I'm serious," she kissed his cheek, opened the door, and was gone.

***

The Ford coasted to a stop before a brownstone in the Bedford-Stuyvesant section of Brooklyn. David switched off the lights and waited, double-parked. A group of men and women emerged from the limo parked up the street. They gathered at the foot of the stairs of one of the buildings for a moment before climbing the steps to the top. There they waited for someone to answer the door. Soon someone did, and the group poured into the building.

David climbed out of his vehicle and closed the distance between himself and the rear of the limo ahead. When he stopped near the trunk, the driver's-side door opened and a burly, barrel-chested black man in a suit and tie exited and approached him menacingly.

"Yo, can I help you?" he asked David in a deep voice.

"Yeah, you can," David said as he pulled out his ID. "I'm David Allerton, a private detective. I need to speak to Two Smooth."

The driver stopped short, and leaned forward to look at the ID, squinting in the near dark. "He's inside the house," he said, guardedly.

"Mind if I cop a squat in the limo?"

He puzzled over the request, as if it were a math question. "I guess so."

"Thanks." David went to the rear passenger-side door and slid into the comfortable vehicle, taking a seat on the side across from the door. When he noticed an ice bucket with a bottle of champagne and then a few fluted glasses in individual holders against the side wall, he took one of the glasses and poured himself a drink. The driver didn't seem to mind, since he just sat quietly glaring at David through the rearview mirror. Finally, David reached into his jacket and withdrew a pack of cigarettes; slipping one between his lips, he raised his lighter to it.

"There's no smoking in the car, mister," the driver said.

"It's alright, Two Smooth won't mind."

Apparently, that was enough reassurance, since the guy relaxed again, letting David smoke in peace. When David stubbed out the cig-arette in an ashtray, he could see people coming down the front steps and approaching the limo door.

As the door opened and Two Smooth leaned over to get in head-first, he stopped short at the threshold of the vehicle when he noticed David sitting inside.

"Who the fuck—?"

David once again flipped open his ID. "I need to speak with you."

Two Smooth glanced at the ID, then looked up at David, smiling broadly, displaying one too many gold teeth. He backed out of the limo and addressed his entourage.

"You motherfuckers stay here," he said as he slipped into the car and closed the door behind him. To the driver, he called out, "Yo! Take a slow one around the block!"

The engine started with a growl.

"What the fuck do you want?" He turned to David.

Two Smooth was a white boy, skinny and clear skinned. Around his neck hung a thick rope of gold, and a wide pair of dark sunglasses obscured his eyes. He wore a New York Yankees cap cocked to the side, a patterned polo shirt under a gray hoodie, baggy jeans and sneakers. Huge diamond-studded gold rings covered his fingers, and he constantly gestured when he talked, no doubt to show them off. He came as a shock to David, who initially thought he'd be a black man like himself when he was tailing his car moments earlier.

"Do you mind if I record us?"

Two Smooth frowned, "For what?"

"It's better than me scribbling in a pad."

Two Smooth thought about it for a moment, then said, "I guess it's alright. Go ahead."

"You knew Hugh Osterman?" David asked as he withdrew the IC recorder from his jacket and turned it on.

"Fuck yeah, bro'. He was my dude. Brother got himself whacked a week ago."

"Just a few days ago actually," David corrected, matter-of-factly. "Do you know of anyone who would have enough of a grudge against him to pop him several times in the chest?"

"Naaah—brother was a pussy. He just did wheeling and dealing, with a fucking attitude. That's why I liked him. He had big balls, but he was a pussy when the shit hit the fan, you know what I mean?"

"Yeah, a lightweight, huh?"

"You got it," Two Smooth pointed at David as he spoke, his rings glittering with the diamonds' refracted light.

"You seem to be doing pretty good for yourself, Two," David said.

"Well, you know how things go." Two Smooth licked his lips and thumbed his nose.

"No, I don't. What exactly is it you do?"

He sat back comfortably. "I network people."

"Yeah. Sell any coke?"

"Naaah, I don't mess with that shit."

"I hear you have a stable of snow bunnies that says otherwise."

He smirked. "Snow bunnies. I don't know any. I hook men and women up, but I don't give a fuck what they do—you know what I mean?"

"A little prostitution there?"

Two Smooth frowned. "What is this? You questioning me about my shit? What the fuck is this? Am I a suspect?"

"No—not yet."

"Fuck, not ever. I don't know shit about who whacked Hugh. I was his business partner, not his bodyguard."

"Could you give me the names of some of his business associates?"

"No, man, that's up to you to find out. I'm not droppin' a dime on my bro'."

"You don't want us to find his killer?"

"I don't want to bust up my network."

"Network, huh?"

"That's right, bro'."

"I see. Well then, Two Smooth, I guess we're done."

"Yeah, my dude, your stop is coming up now."

The limo came to a halt and Two Smooth pointed to the driver's-side rear door. "Go out that way."

David exited the car and shut the door. He watched across the top of the vehicle as the entourage filed inside. Soon the door closed and the limo pulled away, leaving David alone in the street.

***

When David came home, he found Kevin lying across the couch reading what looked to be reports.

"How did it go?" Kevin asked.

"Kinda like a dead end. No promising leads." David rounded the easy chair and fell more than sat in it. "Here, hot off the presses." He leaned forward and tossed a manila envelope onto Kevin's stomach.

"What's this?" Kevin sat further up.

"Transcript. My interview with a motherfucker named Two Smooth."

Kevin, excited now, slipped his legs off the side of the couch, and sat forward to stare wide-eyed at David. "You *met* Two Smooth?"

"Yeah, you heard of him?"

"Yeah, from a snow bunny in MacDonald's home. She was really tying one on when she told me about him."

"Well, I met with him."

"What happened? Any good info?"

"Nothing. Read the transcript."

Kevin handed over to David the reports he'd been reading. "The addresses of the most often called phone numbers."

"This is probably just the surface of Two Smooth's 'network.' "

"Network?"

"Read the transcript."

"So, are we going to split them up?"

"You want to? Feel up to it?" David said as he looked over the names and addresses.

"I'm a detective too, you know. I had the same training and years on the force as you."

"Yeah, so what? Which one of us is more skilled in the field?"

"Let's not talk about that, alright?" Kevin said, getting exasperated.

"It's up to you, boss."

Kevin opened the envelope and looked over the transcript. "He called Osterman a pussy?" Kevin laughed.

"Yeah. Very flamboyant kid."

"Oh—I see. Network."

David stood up and headed for the laser printer to copy the reverse lookup phone records. "I'll go check the top three in the morning."

"Reynolds and Ferryman dropped by this afternoon."

"What did they want? Are they ahead of us?"

"Not that I can tell."

"Good, I hate it when they're ahead."

"Tell me about it," David said as stepped over to Kevin to hand him the original documents. "See ya tomorrow, bro'."

"Yeah, good night."

BORDERING ON THE INSANE

"Certainly, I knew Hugh," the white-haired gentleman said. He sat with Kevin in a crowded Starbucks coffeehouse, with a score of people chattering at the tables around them. He was faultlessly attired in a pinstriped suit, red tie, and cufflinks, and perfectly groomed, with his neatly trimmed beard and not a hair on his head out of place. "He was a friend as well as a business associate."

Kevin found Peter Detroit because his cell phone was registered to his home address. Instead of going directly to his residence, Kevin called him first. Mr. Detroit arranged the meeting at the coffee shop, a place where it was highly unlikely he would be recognized. Kevin also liked the idea because it was someplace public.

"Do you know of anyone who wanted to see him dead?"

"No—well, other than his ex-wife," Detroit laughed.

"Seriously?"

The laugh ended abruptly as he asked, "You're serious, aren't you?"

"Very," Kevin assured him, running his fingers through his dark hair. "Everyone is a suspect now—including you."

"Me? I was his fucking friend."

"Let's get off that. You said his wife?"

"I was just kidding," Detroit asserted.

"Anyone else then?"

Detroit lifted his coffee to his lips and took a sip before continuing.

"He had some chop with a deal that went bad. He kept bitching about it to everyone."

"Know any details?"

"Osterman was making a deal for something from this guy in Brooklyn."

"What was the deal for? You know?"

Detroit swallowed. "Drugs, maybe?"

"Do you *know*?"

"I believe it was drugs. I'm not sure."

"So what happened?"

"Cops busted the shipment. They made it all go away. Something like that. The guy in Brooklyn didn't have his side of the deal anymore. Osterman was pissed because he was a good supplier."

"Makes life a little harder for Osterman."

"I would assume so. He was bitching about getting tighter on the money he had for drugs because of the lack of goods. It seems that everything around him ran on coke."

"You use?" Kevin asked.

Looking very uncomfortable, Detroit answered, "Occasionally."

"Attend any of his snow bunny parties?"

"Sometimes."

"Can you give me the address of this guy in Brooklyn?"

"I wish I could."

"You think *he* whacked Osterman?"

"I think he knows *who* whacked Osterman."

"Can you give me any leads on this person?"

"Not really. Not more than Stew MacDonald could."

The second name on his list was a dead end. Kevin was heated.

The woman knew little more than squat. Either that, or she was holding out. Kevin didn't care which. At least he could still look forward to his interview with Stewart MacDonald. Not finding him at home, he headed for the offices of Osterman-MacDonald.

The impressive futuristic décor of the seventeenth floor office in midtown Manhattan took Kevin by surprise. Business had to be flourishing in order for them to spring for all this luxury, he thought. He strolled past rich leather couches to the large C-shaped reception desk, where a woman wearing a headset looked up at him and said, "Can I help you?"

"I'm here to see Stewart MacDonald."

"Do you have an appointment?"

"No."

"Mr. MacDonald does not see anyone without an appointment."

"You may want to tell him that a Kevin Whitehouse is here to speak to him." Kevin flipped open his ID.

She looked at it for a moment, comparing face to photo, and then pressed a button. "Yes," she said into the mouthpiece. "Mr. Kevin Whitehouse, a private detective, is down here to see you." She paused, then said, "Yes. Yes. Okay."

"Take the elevator to the twenty-first floor. He will be waiting," she said.

Thanks," Kevin turned and headed for the elevator. When it stopped on the twenty-first floor, he was greeted by a tall lanky, dark-haired man in a white polo shirt, khakis and loafers. Around his neck was a thin gold chain.

"Stewart MacDonald," he strode over to Kevin, shaking his hand. The man was handsome, had no facial hair, was mature in years, with lines just beginning to form at the corners of his eyes and mouth. His hair already betrayed a few strands of gray. Kevin surveyed the entire floor behind him—MacDonald's office—which was expansive and pristine, as if entering into a huge medical examination hall.

"Thank you for seeing me, Mr. MacDonald."

"Please, please, come in." MacDonald waved him through the doorway, guiding him with a hand at his back into what looked like a living room area, and gestured to a sofa. "Have a seat."

Kevin sat down.

MacDonald walked across the room to a gleaming marble-topped bar and asked, "Would you like a drink?"

"Soda?"

"Oh, right," MacDonald chuckled. "No drinking on the job."

Kevin remained silent.

"You're not a cop, though. Because I spoke to the police already," he said to Kevin as he went behind the bar to look for some soda. "Cola?"

"That's fine."

MacDonald came away with two cans—handing one to Kevin—and sat down in a loveseat nearby so he could face him.

"No," Kevin said, "I'm not the police, just a private dick."

"So I really don't have to answer any of your questions, right?"

"This is true, but that might seem like you're hiding something, and we do work closely with the police."

"I see," MacDonald popped the top of his cola.

"Do you mind if I record us?"

"No, not at all."

Kevin turned on the IC recorder and rested it on the sofa next to him. "You and Osterman were partners for how long?"

"Hell," MacDonald smiled, "for something like twenty-five years."

"You guys were pretty close with Two Smooth Williams?"

"You know about him?"

"We know just about everything, Mr. MacDonald, and we'll soon know who Osterman's killer was."

"That's a good thing, Mr. Whitehouse."

"That's only if we get help from people like you, Mr. MacDonald. That's why it's very important that you cooperate."

"Go ahead with your questions, detective."

"What do you know about Two Smooth Williams?"

"A mutual partner of ours. We manage his holdings."

"You manage more than his holdings, don't you? You help him launder money."

"You could say that."

"What does he traffic in, Mr. MacDonald? Coke and prostitution?"

"Yeah," said MacDonald, and then added anxiously, "Look, we were involved only marginally, detective."

"I really don't care about all that. That's a separate investigation—if there will ever be one. Right now I want to know, how did you guys get your hands on the coke for Two Smooth to sell?"

"Through a guy named Chase Arthur."

"Chase live in Brooklyn?"

"Yeah, how did you know that?"

"I can read minds. Go on."

"Well, it's pretty straightforward. Chase would get the cocaine, bring it to us. We paid him with securities that he then sold and cashed through the market to turn the drugs into money for himself. Then Two Smooth would sell the coke for us, and we'd divide the profits."

"And the prostitution?"

"Two Smooth's side gig. He pimps out these cokeheads, and we use them at parties. They are some pretty wild women when you get them all hopped up." MacDonald was smiling broadly as he said this, obviously basking in some fond recollections.

"Do you think that Two Smooth has the motive and the where-withal to murder Osterman?"

"Oh, no," MacDonald shook his head, sitting back. "Oh, no. Two

Smooth and Hugh were close. We were more than business partners, we were friends."

"With a two-bit pimp and pusher?"

"Well, that's a very negative view of him."

"Isn't that the only way to view him, Mr. MacDonald?"

"Well, if you're asking me if Two could kill Hugh, I'd say no way."

"What was this altercation that Chase was having with Osterman?"

"Hugh was hot because he had promised people shipments…"

"I thought that Two Smooth moved the shit?"

"He did, but Hugh started moving it around in the office, and to his friends. He got a pretty wide circle of businessmen hooked on the stuff. He started becoming their supplier—by default."

"So he promised his friends, now his connects, shit in the mail and the post office closed."

"So to speak. Chase was hit by the police who confiscated his supply. He got away, but a lot of shit was seized."

"Osterman was left out in the cold."

"His connects started to pressure him for their supply and he didn't have it."

"Could one of his connects whack him because of that?"

MacDonald shrugged. "Could be. Maybe got together and hired a hit man to whack him for not coming through. I don't know. That would be pretty extreme, though."

"How about Chase. Could he do it?"

"Chase?" MacDonald seriously pondered the question. "I don't think so. Two Smooth and Hugh were his biggest movers. He'd be cutting off his nose to spite his face."

"I guess you're right about that."

"It could be one of his connects."

"Where would they get the muscle from? They know people?

They're businessmen, not gangsters."

"They're connected obliquely to Two and Chase because a lot of Osterman's people used to come to Two Smooth's parties. They would mingle with thugs there. Maybe they connected with one of them."

"This is different. This thug Osterman knew. After all, he let him in."

"In?"

"Osterman lived in a gated residence. The killer had to have been announced from the gate, because the butler opened the door for him. Then he joined Osterman in the kitchen and they walked to the pool area together. Even Osterman's squeeze didn't run when she saw the killer."

"Amazing. Well, I can only imagine that they met up with a thug at one of these parties. Someone acquainted with Osterman and the one who gave the orders."

"Possibly."

"Those parties were more like orgies," MacDonald admitted.

"Describe one."

"Women fucking all over the place. Some of us got high with the black thugs and the white suits. Hell, we even fucked together. We were like blood brothers. It would have been easy for Osterman to come upon his killer there. The both of them probably fucking the same woman, giving each other high fives…"

"I get the picture. Do you know where I can find this Chase?"

"Yes. I'll give you his address."

MacDonald stood up and strode over to his desk in the distance. Kevin shook his hand, finally a solid lead. He was ahead of David, Ferryman and Reynolds. He was going to crack this case first. He could feel it.

MacDonald returned with the address written on a piece of paper. Kevin looked at it. "Where is this at?"

"North Crown Heights."

"Bad neighborhood, huh?"

"You wouldn't want to park your Mercedes there."

The Desert Eagle pistol barked seven times in rapid succession, and then was silent. The trim blonde woman popped its clip, broke it apart on a small table next to her, coming away with the barrel, the body, and the firing mechanism. David watched her from the other side of the table, wearing a pair of bulbous ear protectors on his head. They stood together in an underground firing range. The curvaceous sharpshooter was one of the numbers on his cell phone list.

"They were moving the shit from Colombia," Claire Montague said. "Hugh got a kick out of moving whole kilos past us. The more money you had, the more you gravitated to Hugh."

"Where were you in his orbit?"

"I was sucking Hugh's cock. I was in so deep I should have had a respirator."

"So, what happened?"

Claire went to a box of bullets and one by one, reloaded the clip. "He was getting his shit from Chase, who was moving some really enormous weight…" Her voice trailed off. "Are you a cop?"

"I would be crazy to go up against a woman who could handle a Desert Eagle like you can," David said with a hearty grin.

She pressed the big, red recall button on the partition wall. There was a whirring sound and in seconds the paper target was before her. She tore it loose from its hooks and passed it over to David, who righted it in his hands. It was the dark outline of an assailant pointing a gun. The target zeroed in on a bull's-eye in the center mass. Her bullets ripped through it in a close grouping.

"Pretty impressive at full auto," David said. "Can you do that single shot?"

"I never fire single shot," Claire replied.

"Well, tell me now, Chase was moving enormous weight."

"Are you sure you aren't a cop?"

"I'm a dick, I told you that."

She looked at him incredulously.

"Would a brother lie to you?" he asked.

"First, you gotta show me one."

David smirked at her response. "You said Chase was moving serious weight, right?"

"Yes," she continued. "He was moving tractor trailers full of this shit. Serious weight and Hugh seemed to have most of Wall Street hooked. He had his little bitches selling at parties, and these parties were the rave."

"Have you ever been to one?"

"Several."

"What were they like?"

"A lot of drinking, toking, snorting, and fucking."

"Fucking."

"I had my first gangbang while there."

David blinked.

"So," Claire said, "I was with Hugh when he got the bad news from one of Chase's stooges. A major shipment had been picked up by the cops. Chase got away with his hide. Some of his guys were nabbed, and everyone was afraid that they would squeal."

"What happened to the deal?"

"It fell through. Chase didn't have the coke for Hugh and Hugh was hip deep in requests. There were a lot of people really strung out, demanding that Hugh come up with something—anything."

"And?"

"Hugh came up empty-handed." Claire took another target sheet from a box under the table, hooked it on the retaining hooks and punched the recall button, sending the target away. "He didn't have their shit. The pressure was on. Hugh's contacts were pressuring him for their coke, Hugh was pressuring Chase, Chase was pressuring Colombia—"

"And the Colombians?"

"They thought it was a big fucking joke." Claire reassembled the Desert Eagle. "They couldn't care less about the demands of a bunch of white boys in suits on Wall Street."

"But they were no doubt pissed about the seizure."

"Yes, they were. They thought Chase untrustworthy."

"Go on."

Claire turned to face the firing range. She took the Desert Eagle in both hands and fired a shot, followed by a pause, and then another shot, until she emptied the weapon. "Hugh saw it as his chance to make a move. He went over Chase's head and straight to his supplier, claiming he could move their shit better and safer than Chase."

"Fuck out of here. How did Hugh know how to contact these South Americans?"

"Chase was dumb enough to take him on a drop. There was a meet. Hugh, being the businessman, got their contact information."

"Yeah, he sounds like a real businessman," David said sarcastically.

"Hugh couldn't be fucked with, Mr. Allerton."

"Especially with you on his cock."

"Whatever." She turned to the table again, disassembling the Desert Eagle once more and removing its clip. "Anyway, the Colombians saw a safer deal in Hugh, whereas Chase saw a betrayal."

"Could Chase have killed Hugh over this move?"

"I doubt it. Chase is not that type of person. Then again, you never know. Chase did run around with some scary types."

"How do you know?"

"They came to the parties. Dark, sinister motherfuckers who wouldn't get high—or even fuck. They would just exist."

"Security."

"Maybe," she punched the red button. The whirring sound filled the air once more. "I doubt it, though. These guys didn't take orders."

"Other dealers then?"

"I don't know," Claire replied as the target stopped next to her. She tore it away and handed it to David. He held it up. The grouping was the same, tightly knit around the center mass.

"Alright, so you've made your point," David said handing the target back. "Maybe one of his strung-out cokeheads planted Hugh."

"Wall Street white boys? I don't think so." Claire crumpled up the target and tossed it to the side.

"Well, someone did."

Claire hunched her shoulders. "It's possible they hired a hit man."

"No, this guy was someone Osterman knew. Someone not all that professional. And the way you describe these *parties*, I would guess that this guy was strung out on some great coke, since he couldn't pass up the chance to fuck Osterman's snow bunny. I don't think a professional would have wasted his time doing that."

"If he was horny."

"He'd go home and fuck his girlfriend. How long would you hang around a house full of corpses, when anyone could come in?"

"Good point."

"No, this guy wasn't all that skilled, but he was well known to Hugh's household, and had a real grudge against him."

"So you think it was Chase?"

"On second thought, I don't think so either. He would be too obvious. Chase probably realized he'd be a prime suspect. That's why he wouldn't have done anything. Not even hire someone to do it for him."

"So how are you going to find the person who did it? I mean, where do you start if the person who ordered the hit keeps his mouth shut?"

David smiled. "You never get to the person that ordered the hit until you get to the person that did the hit. When they fess up, you've got your man."

"Really?"

"Well, Ms. Montague. I need some contact information on these Wall Street guys, and this Chase character. Can you do that for me?"

"I'm not finking on innocent people, sheriff."

"I'm not the heat. As I told you before, I'm a private dick. I don't care about who fucked whom or who snorted what. I want to find Osterman's killer. That's all."

"No… that's bullshit. You share information with the police. They know what you know, that's why they get you guys involved in the first place."

"No—" David shook his head. "No, that's not true."

Claire rested her gun on the table and stared into David's eyes, looking for the lie.

Kevin picked up the interview with Claire Montague. "You want to include this transcript with the rest of the material I'm giving Ferryman and Reynolds?"

"Yeah," David, stretched out on the couch, replied lazily.

There was a knock.

"That's probably them now."

"Whatever," David said. He busied himself with a can of suds on the coffee table.

Kevin crossed the room and opened the front door. It was Ferryman. His narrow features were fraught with concern. "Whitehouse?"

"Ferryman," Kevin opened the door. "Come on in."

"How are you, buddy?" Ferryman said as he stepped inside, while Reynolds stayed on the threshold, holding open the door.

"Good, I have your shit right here. Wanna stay for a while?"

Ferryman took the envelope and opened it. "Naaah, we have to keep moving to One Police Plaza this afternoon."

"S'up, Ferryman!" David called, raising his hand.

"We have a meeting about this case," Ferryman said to Kevin, ignoring David.

"David just said hi, George," Kevin said with some concern.

Reynolds broke out into a fit of laughter, leaving the doorway and staggering down the hallway, allowing the door to slowly close. Kevin glanced his way, and then back to Ferryman, who waved reluctantly, "S'up, David?"

"You know, Ferryman, you need to bury the hatchet," Kevin persisted.

"I've got to go," Ferryman said in reply. He reached out to grip Kevin's shoulder, firmly, warmly. They remained silent for a few minutes, listening to Reynolds, who was still laughing behind the door.

"What's with him?" Kevin asked, gesturing with his head to the closed door.

"He thinks you're playing games."

"What? I don't get it."

"Forget about him," Ferryman released Kevin, and waved the envelope. "Thanks for this."

"Don't mention it."

As Ferryman opened the door and walked out into the hall, he turned to Reynolds and said, "Why don't you shut the fuck up?"

Kevin shut the door behind them.

"You see," David rolled over on the couch, facing Kevin. "That's why I don't talk to those motherfuckers anymore."

"You're just antisocial."

"Fuck that. And who did you give my book to?"

Kevin walked over to the desk and took a seat. "What book are you talking about?"

"The one that was sitting right there," David sat up to point at the bookshelf. "Before you moved the books around so I wouldn't notice."

"I gave your sailing book to Reynolds."

"You mean the laughing clown in the hallway?"

"The laughing clown."

"What the fuck you do that for? I don't do shit for those cockroaches. They're your friends—lend them your shit."

"Whatever."

"Jefferies is it. He's the only one I'm dealing with, because he gives a real shit about us. He gives us cases."

"Which he's not supposed to be doing."

"So?"

"So we have to deal with Ferryman and Reynolds. They could bitch about us working this case if they wanted to."

"You're handing it to them," David said with some anger evident in his tone. "You're handing them our work as if it was Halloween candy."

"We're sharing information."

"And what are they sharing with us? They're two-bit flatfoots. Shit-kicking pieces of garbage. They'll just swoop in and take credit for our moves. They're a bunch of users, and they're just using us... using *you*."

"Jefferies knows otherwise."

"That's why I'll only deal with his ass."

There was a pause in the conversation as Kevin checked his laptop.

David groaned, climbing up off the couch and stepping over to the closet. "I'm going to Brooklyn to see this Chase motherfucker tonight."

"Why do you have to go at night?"

"I move better in the night. Besides, criminals act up more after dark, because they think the entire world does a nine to five." He opened the closet door and reached in behind the clothes that hung there. "They think we think crime goes to sleep at night. I'm there to answer that."

"Alright, big bad daddy. I'll hold down the fort."

"Fuck that. Don't you want to come along?"

"Can I?" Kevin turned to him, trying to mask his excitement.

Having found what he wanted, David straightened up—he was holding a Remington 12-gauge shotgun. "Fuck, what kind of question is that?"

"Do you absolutely have to bring that?"

"This is not a social call. This Chase might not want me there."

"So, you'll make your presence known, I'm sure."

"Don't I always, Kev? Now do you want to come, or would you rather stay home and read a transcript?" David reached up to the top shelf of the closet and came away with a box of shells. He sat back down on the couch, with the shotgun across his lap, checking the safety.

"You think he has something to do with the murder?" Kevin asked, turning his full attention from the laptop to David.

"I think he'll have goons around him." David opened the box of shells, set it down next to him and began loading the gun. "And I think he'll be surrounded by more guns than my little peashooter."

"You're not expecting me to carry anything, are you?"

"Nope. Not at all. I just want you to chill out in the background and let me do all the work, as fucking usual."

***

"Who wants to know?" the peephole said.

David stepped back and put the muzzle of the shotgun over the hole. Kevin stood with his back to the wall, next to the door, his eyes popping wide. "What the fuck?" he hissed.

The door jerked open, "Who the *fuck* is covering my peep—" The tall black male who emerged stopped short when he found himself suddenly face to face with the muzzle of a weapon. He froze, eyes wide, mouth agape.

"Yeah, motherfucker," David nodded with a menacing smile. "Turn around, get down on your knees and assume the position."

The thug complied.

David lowered the weapon and handcuffed him with his hands behind his back, and helped position him so he was lying face down, just inside the apartment. Then he and Kevin stepped gingerly over the prone body and closed the door so that anyone trying to enter would trip over the thug's body. "If I hear this door open or close—if I hear a peep out of you, I'll be back shooting," David whispered.

The thug nodded.

David and Kevin found themselves in a small living room where a cartoon show was in progress on the TV. The room was decorated with cheap paintings on the wall, an empty bookshelf, a stereo, a nondescript sculpture, sofas, chairs, and a PlayStation with its controllers snaked out on the floor.

"Who is it, T-Snuff?" a voice called out from a room off the hallway ahead.

David set off in that direction with his shotgun raised, sighting down its length. He stopped at the opened door to the bathroom on his right, and searched the small room briefly with the muzzle of his gun.

"Don't make me—" said the same voice, but this time it clearly came from the bedroom ahead, where the door was closed.

David first opened the door to a closet on the left, searching it with the gun muzzle, before approaching the door at the end of the hall and kicking it open. An angry, naked man stood on the other side, his anger changing to fear in seconds once he beheld the gun pointing in his direction.

"Get back into bed," David ordered.

"*Fuck!*" the pale-bodied man responded as he staggered backward. The foot of the bed struck the back of his knees, sending him seated on the mattress. The woman on the bed had by this time covered herself with the sheets, and curled her legs up.

While Kevin stood nervously in the doorway, David searched the room and the closets, the muzzle of the shotgun again serving as a probe, but found no one.

"What the fug?" Chase asked David.

After searching through the room, David tossed the shotgun to Kevin.

Suddenly, Chase went white-hot heat, crawling backward into the arms of his woman in sheer panic screaming, "*What the fuck do you want?!*"

"I want information, motherfucker," David demanded, going to the foot of the bed, standing before them with Kevin directly behind him. "I want to know who whacked Osterman."

"*How am I to know?*" Chase shouted back. His hair was a wild tangle, his eyes wide as saucers with fright.

"Don't yell at me," David said calmly. "I want answers. I'm not interested in killing you."

"You bust into my crib and start throwing guns the fuck around. You're crazy, man, what the fuck do you think I'm thinking?"

"You were moving dope for Osterman," David persisted, ignoring Chase's remarks.

"*Osterman!* That fuck jerked me."

"With the Colombians."

"Goddamn right."

"And you didn't like that."

"*No*, I didn't."

"So, you had one of your soul brothers do him in."

"Oh hell, no. My people don't kill. We don't fuck with weapons like you do."

"And the reason for that?"

"More jail time… What are you? A cop?"

"Don't worry about what I am," David growled back. "You are moving weight. I want to know what happened after Osterman jerked you."

"He jerked me. That's all."

"That's all? You didn't go to the Colombians? Liar!"

"Yes, yes, I did that!" Chase corrected. "I went to the Colombians as soon as I knew he jerked me. I begged them to give me another chance. They said they would, if I replaced their one hundred kilos. *One hundred kilos!* How the fuck do I do that?"

"Put bullets into Osterman for revenge."

"How is that shit going to get me my one hundred kilos?"

"Let me explain it to you, genius. The Colombians trust Osterman enough to give him a heavy shipment. You find it, whack him, and take his shipment back to the Colombians. Paid in fucking full."

Chase thought that over for a second or two. "But that's not what happened."

"Convince me otherwise."

The words "*Freeze, Motherfucker!*" were suddenly heard from the doorway. David frowned as he glanced over his shoulder to see a scruffy looking black male, armed with *his shotgun.*

How in the fuck? David thought for an instant.

The intruder shouted, "Put your—"

David charged backward, so the shotgun muzzle went over his shoulder as he plowed into him. The gun went off, firing loudly, tearing a hole in the ceiling. Both men fell into the hall, with David atop his adversary, the shotgun flying away. Wasting no time, David delivered several harsh elbow jabs into the guy's midsection, then leaped to his feet and trained his Saturday night special from his belt holster down on his stunned foe.

"Now, don't *you* move," David panted. Remembering Chase, he turned and pointed the gun at him, still on his bed, then looked around, finding Kevin in the bathroom, sitting quietly on the edge of the tub.

"*Kevin! What the fuck are you doing?*" David gasped.

"I heard him coming, so I ducked in here," Kevin replied calmly.

"For what fucking reason, Kevin? You were supposed to have my goddamn back!"

"I just—" his voice faltered.

"How did he get the shotgun from you, Kevin?"

"I must have dropped it in the hallway."

Throughout the interchange, David had dropped the muzzle of his gun down to the chin of the man at his feet. "Kevin, give me your set of cuffs."

Kevin went through his pockets and checked his belt. "Shit, Dave, I must have left them home."

"You are fucking useless tonight, brother." David reached for the spare pair on his belt. "Here, put these on," he said to the guy on the ground as he dropped the handcuffs on his belly. He hastily donned the jewelry. David kicked at the cuff on his right wrist, and commanded, "Tight, motherfucker."

"Okay, okay!" he replied, tightening both cuffs.

David gestured to the shotgun further down the hall with the Special in his hand. He then pointed it back down at the perpetrator on the floor at his feet. "Let me hear or catch you crawling for that shotgun and you'll see how hot thirty-eight slugs are when they dig into your ass. You got me?"

The assailant nodded fearfully.

David stepped from the hall to the bedroom, keeping his pistol pointed at Chase, who crawled backward, trapping his girl between himself and the headboard.

"*You are fucking crazy, man!*" Chase screamed.

"I want information and I want it now!" David retorted, angrily.

"What do you want?" Chase held up a frightened hand to the muzzle of the Saturday Night Special. "Please, for god's sake, put that thing down! I'm unarmed, man!"

"Did you kill Osterman?"

"Fuck no, man! That's what I've been trying to tell you! I let Osterman walk because there was nothing I could do. Besides, I heard that he asked for my weight and didn't get it," Chase resumed.

"He asked for your weight?"

"Yeah, he asked for a hundred keys. He got fifty," Chase said, almost whining now.

"Not enough to cover demand."

"Hell, no. He was short. Short big time. You should question his contacts. Not me. He had to prove himself to the Colombians. He needed more. He came to me for help."

"And you helped him?"

"Fuck no—I wouldn't give him my dick. I told him to go die." Chase quickly corrected himself with an angry shake of his head, "I mean, I told him to go fuck himself."

David stewed as the tired wail of a siren filled the air.

"If you're not a cop," Chase said, "you'd better run."

"I'm a cop."

"Fuck, you are the strangest goddamn cop I've ever seen."

"You're not a cop," Jefferies said as he and David sat facing each other in one of the interrogation rooms. Just two chairs, a desk and an overhead light. "You can't just go into someone's house without a search warrant and demand information from them. It just doesn't work that way."

"I know how it works, Jefferies."

"No, you don't," Jefferies replied grimly. "You're going to face charges for this— investigation or not. I have to charge you with a crime."

"That's alright, like I give a fuck."

"Where's Kevin?"

"He's not here."

Jefferies sat back in his chair across from David and sighed. "Well, for all of your troubles, what have you found out?"

"This guy, Chase, was moving cocaine in mass quantities. You need to lean on him to get his network."

"I'm not concerned with his *network*, David. I'm concerned about you and Kevin."

"What the fuck are you concerned about us for? We're doing our job."

Jefferies looked saddened as he said, "You need help, David. I think you're out of control."

"I just went in—"

"You just went into an innocent man's home, roughed up and handcuffed his friends, and terrorized his woman."

"His friends? His friends?" David slid his chair back, stood and struck the tabletop with his fist. "That motherfucker is guilty. He's a mule for the cartel—" David thought about it for a moment and added, "Well, maybe *was*."

"See?" Jefferies said, making a dismissive gesture with his hand. "You don't even know if he's guilty or not."

"I know he's guilty." David said. "He told me himself."

"Under duress. You had a gun on him. I'd confess to killing Osterman myself."

"Bullshit."

"He's changing his story right now. He has his lawyer with a hand up his ass, telling him what to say like a puppet. Even his girlfriend is singing a canary tune to implicate you."

David's hand went to his chest in defense. "*I* was almost shot—"

"With your own shotgun!"

"I gave it to Kevin."

"Well, that obviously didn't work."

"I guess the fuck not."

Jefferies stood up from his chair, sighing with a level of despair. "I'm not charging you, David. I'm trying to give you an idea of how this could have gone. Just don't do this shit again. I don't know what Chase Arthur's lawyer is going to ask for. I would suppose nothing since he's pretty glad his client hasn't been caught with several keys of cocaine. He wants him out. That's all he's spouting right now… so you get to walk."

"That works for me, Sam," David said as he turned to leave.

"Don't let this shit happen again."

"It won't."

"So, do you think this guy has anything to do with Osterman's murder?"

Near the door, David turned around to answer Jefferies' question. "Chase Arthur is not the killer."

"How can you tell?"

"He would have confessed—because he's weak. He's just a dope dealer, not a killer. And as I've been told, he's just not someone who would order a hit."

"You can tell all that by waving a shotgun at him?"

"I didn't wave a shotgun at him."

"So he didn't fess up. What's next?"

"I don't know. I'm out of leads."

"I find that hard to believe."

"I've got a feeling that I've walked right past the killer. Can I get out of here now?"

"Have you seen Dr. Fagen yet?"

David paused. "No."

"You changed addresses on him."

"I moved. That's right."

"You stopped seeing him. I asked."

"Sam, you're in my business."

Jefferies exhaled tiredly—exhausted by the conversation—and headed in David's direction. "No static, no static. Let me get you out of here."

WAKING UP TO THE MADNESS

When David entered the apartment, he found Kevin standing in the living room in his underwear.

"Where the fuck were you?" David asked accusingly.

"They didn't charge me. I was never picked up," Kevin explained with an innocent air.

"What's up with you and my back?"

"What do you mean?"

David approached his friend slowly, eyes narrowed. "I gave you the fucking shotgun, Kevin. You are supposed to watch my back, not hide in the fucking bathroom."

As David drew closer, Kevin spoke faster. "You were out of control, David. You were threatening deadly force without cause, for Chrissakes."

"Fuck that, Kevin. I had a shotgun aimed at my back. I don't like when dangerous felons aim a shotgun at my back."

"That guy wouldn't have shot you."

"Tell that to the ceiling that took a half ounce of buckshot."

"You're overreacting. You're—"

David charged into Kevin, plowing him backward into his computer desk, then pushing him down into his chair, his hands clutching at his neck. Kevin struggled upward and pushed back. Both men staggered around in an odd tango into the bookshelves on the side wall. Books rained down on them as Kevin head-butted David into the far corner of the living room.

David finally broke away and with one hand thrust Kevin back, while he cocked his other hand into a fist aimed at his friend's face.

Suddenly, there was a piercing scream that caused both men to freeze in place.

Margaret stood in the center of the living room wrapped in nothing but a bed sheet. "What is wrong with you two?" she exclaimed.

"Just having a talk," Kevin panted. "Go back into the bedroom."

"A talk?"

"Yeah, nothing to be concerned about—"

David interrupted Kevin to say, "Your boyfriend almost got me killed last night."

"Kevin?" Margaret asked.

"He's exaggerating," Kevin said, stomping past David and heading for the kitchen. "Did you at least record the conversation?"

"Yeah, motherfucker." David retrieved his IC recorder from his jacket. "It was in my pocket the whole time."

There was a knock on the door. Margaret dashed into the bedroom, while Kevin, still clad in his underwear, peeked out from the kitchen. David went to the door to peer through the peephole, and then opened the door.

"Hello," said their caller, a man stood there, neatly attired, with a graying beard and curly red hair.

"Dr. Fagen." David stepped back, allowing him to enter.

"Kevin?"

"No, David."

"*David!* Why yes, of course," Dr. Fagen said as he entered the living room, stepping over the mound of books that had fallen to the floor, behaving like their presence was nothing unusual. "How have you been doing?"

"Good, doc."

"You moved since the last time we met."

"Yeah—it was Kevin's idea."

"Kevin thought of it, huh?"

"Yes, he did."

Dr. Fagen sat down carefully on the sofa. David took a seat in a straight-backed chair across from him. "So what's up, doc?"

Fagen stared at David with a concerned expression through his gold wire-rimmed glasses as he spoke. "Jefferies gave me your new address. He thought you might need help."

"I'm fine, doc."

"He felt you were 'acting out' again."

"Acting out?"

"How do you feel, David?"

"I feel fine, doc. What's the matter with *you*?"

"Nothing, my friend."

"Jefferies got you over here because he thinks I still need help. But I'm fine."

"No, David, you are *not* fine."

David frowned. "What the fuck are you talking about, dude?"

"You've stopped taking your Abilify, haven't you?"

"I don't need it."

Fagen settled himself on the couch and crossed his legs. "Describe yourself, David."

"What?"

"Describe yourself."

"What are you talking about, doc? You see me. What do I look like to you?"

"But you don't *see* yourself." The doctor pulled out his cell phone from his jacket pocket and held it up, taking a snapshot of David. "Go ahead. Describe yourself."

"This is ridiculous—"

"Humor me."

David sighed as he sat back in his chair. "I'm a black man, tall and well built, ex-Marine, ex-martial arts expert, and handsome as a motherfucker." He turned smugly to the side to show Dr. Fagen his profile, thumbing his chin with his thumb and forefinger. "I'm clean shaven—"

Doctor Fagen leaned forward as he held up the small screen of the cell phone. David looked at the photo. It was a picture of Kevin.

David frowned. "I don't understand, doc." He took the cell phone and stared at the screen. "Something is wrong."

"Nothing is wrong, Kevin." Dr. Fagen reached over to retrieve his cell phone from David. "Your name is Kevin Whitehouse. You suffer from Multiple Personality Disorder."

"What?" David shook his head, genuinely confused. "You've got to be kidding me, doc."

"You have a problem, Kevin. You think you are two different people, and I've been treating you for this disorder for the past two years—ever since your nervous breakdown. Do you remember that, Kevin? The nervous breakdown?"

David stood up, thought furiously for a moment, and then headed for the kitchen, finding it empty save for the case file material on the table. "Kevin?"

He could hear the doctor calling him from the living room. "You will not find him in there, Kevin," Fagen said. "*You* are Kevin."

David came back into the living room, angry now. "You've got this all wrong, doc. Very wrong!" He crossed the room on his way to Kevin's bedroom. He kicked open the door, but found the room empty, the bed unmade, the sheets all tousled.

"Margaret?" David scanned the room briefly. "Where are you, bitch?"

"Margaret?" Dr. Fagen repeated from behind him. "You're getting worse, Kevin. Now it appears that you've created a third personality."

"*No!*" David turned to the doctor, returning to the living room. "No, I haven't. You're fucking with my mind. You're the one who's making all of this shit up." David began to pace and, in his distress, started pulling at his short cropped Afro. "You're confusing me. You're a professional. You know how to screw with people's gray matter."

"Kevin, you are not in full possession of your faculties. You need help. You need to resume your medication. You need therapy as well."

"Fuck that shit." David stopped in his tracks to face the doctor. "I have a gun in the closet. You'd better leave."

"Kevin, you're not—"

"*Stop calling me Kevin!*" David screamed. "Get out of my crib or I swear I'll bust a cap in you."

The doctor paused for a moment before he said, "You want me to leave?"

"Yes. Get the fuck out of here." David returned to the straight-backed chair and fell into it, looking dejected. He inhaled deeply, then exhaled before he said, "I'm not going to fight with you any longer, doc. I'm just telling you to leave."

Dr. Fagen reached into his jacket and produced his business card, placing it on the coffee table near the couch. "Look, Kevin—"

"*David!*" he snarled, not even looking up as he said it.

"David, then. Get in touch with me. Let's talk. You'll go through a period of confusion after this. It's understandable and expected—but I can help you. I really can."

"Goodbye, doctor," David said with a distinct edge of finality in his voice.

As Dr. Fagen stood at the front door, his hand on the knob, he glanced back for one last parting shot. "You were always a good person, David. You're not some kind of freak. You just need professional help. Your personality will continue to fragment until we lose you forever. Do you understand me?"

He paused, waiting for David to respond. When he didn't, the doctor finally left the apartment, closing the door softly behind him.

"Is he gone?" Kevin asked from the kitchen.

"Where the fuck was you?"

"I was standing right next to the refrigerator—well, maybe a little behind it."

"What the fuck for? You heard the doc calling me you."

Kevin emerged from the kitchen and headed for the couch, where he stretched out full length. "The doc is cracked. That's why I wanted to move in the first place. He was becoming a nuisance."

"He was, wasn't he?" David said. "That little crackpot."

Suddenly Margaret appeared from the hallway leading to the bedrooms, fully dressed in a business suit and light jacket. She crossed in front of them to snatch up her purse from an end table and then hurried to the door.

"And where were you the whole time the good doctor was here?"

David asked.

"I was in the closet, David. I had no clothes on," she said as she reached the door. "You two psychos can go ahead and kill each other now that I'm leaving." In the next instant, she was gone, slamming the door behind her.

"So, what now?" Kevin asked.

David rubbed his eyes with a thumb and forefinger. "We have no more leads, nothing solid."

"Let me ask you: who is the beneficiary of Osterman's death benefits?"

"His ex-wife." David, finally starting to relax, leaned back in his chair and stretched.

"I think one of us should talk to her."

"You do it. Maybe she won't hold your shotgun at your back."

"You're not going to let that rest are you?"

"Why should I, Kevin? I was almost shot in the back of the head."

Kevin shook his head as he asked, "If I'm talking to the old lady, what will you be doing?"

"Interviewing some of the Wall Street punks who attended the parties. Maybe they'll have some leads on Osterman's killer. Claire Montague indicated there were some pretty shady motherfuckers."

"Good luck with that." Kevin rolled over on the couch, turning his back on David, and closed his eyes.

Kevin put the IC recorder into his shirt pocket after turning it on, and trailed behind the woman who wore nothing more than a teddy beneath a silken robe, martini glass in hand. Her hair looked like it was freshly styled from an expensive salon.

"Isn't it too early for drinks?" Kevin asked.

"I don't look at the clock," she replied. "Besides, is this about a police investigation or my personal habits?"

Kevin nodded silently as they entered a huge den furnished with floor-to-ceiling bookshelves—equipped with two sliding ladders to access the topmost shelves—a spacious brocade sofa with matching loveseats, Persian throw rugs and a delft-tiled fireplace. The tall, leggy brunette went straight to the bar on the right, and standing over a silver frosted pitcher, refreshed her drink.

"Can I please have your full name?" Kevin asked.

"Deborah Karen Hendricks." She turned around and leaned back against the bar with a sigh. The years had not been kind to her features, which were not aging gracefully. Her eyes were tired and bloodshot, while there were deep frown lines etched at the corners of her mouth. She still had a good build—and was sexy, even—as was amply demonstrated by the body-skimming lingerie she wore. "No, I didn't kill my ex."

"I wasn't about to ask you that, Ms. Hendricks. Rather, would you happen to know anyone who would?" Kevin asked as he glanced around the room, taking in the details of her lavish surroundings.

"Everyone, if you ask me," she said, taking a sip from her glass. "You want one?"

"No, thank you," Kevin said. "How did you feel about your husband's uh… well, proclivities? Did you even know about them?"

"You mean, about him being found with a skank? I knew he liked cheap women. We were still together when he was having these so-called parties. When we started swinging at these affairs, that's when our marriage started to crumble. He just got too involved with those little tramps and forgot about me."

"So you went to these parties?"

"Yeah," she yawned. "I used to go to them. At first, they were small and private, until some hip-hop type came onboard and brought these prostitutes with him. Next thing you know, it was a packed house. So much so, that my ex and his business partner bought a nightclub."

"The Midnight."

"That's right."

"Did you know that your ex-husband was also selling cocaine?"

"Selling coke? I was one of his biggest customers. He even paid some of his alimony in fucking coke."

"I see," Kevin nodded. "I just have to say that you have the most to gain from his death, Ms. Hendricks."

"So what? So does his fucking partner. He stands to take full control of their company, and his dealer friend gets to run the entire coke business again. Have you ever thought of that?"

"We looked into that."

"Well, you didn't look hard enough if you're in my home asking me if I killed him for his estate."

"So, who would you put your money on as the killer?"

"The dope fiends," she replied without skipping a beat. She took another sip of her martini before adding, "I have a feeling you're grasping at straws here, officer. You are no closer to the killer than you were when you started—right?"

"We're still doing interviews," he replied. "Would you mind if we took a look at your phone records?"

"Why? I'm not in trouble here, am I?"

"No, it's just procedure."

She thought about it, and then shrugged her shoulders. "What the fuck."

"Did you ever meet the dead girl? Ms. Walker?"

"I met with all of those skuzzy tramps. They walked around the parties as if they owned them. Done-up cokeheads, they'd do anything for a line."

"Would you say that you were the same?"

"I had class, Mr.—"

"Private detective Whitehouse."

"Yeah, you told me that. Look detective, if that's all the questions—"

"One more. At these parties, did you ever witness a group of particularly shady types there?"

"Shady types, like who? What?"

"That's what I'm asking you."

"Well, there were bodyguards there, big muscled men in suits. I guess they weren't paid to mingle in the parties because they didn't."

"No, I'm not talking about security; I'm talking about another type of partygoer. The person relating the information could tell the difference between security and partygoers."

Ms. Hendricks thought about it for a moment. "There were these rival groups of Colombians there."

"Rival Colombians?"

"They started coming to the parties, well-dressed men, strictly business."

"Why do you call them rival Colombians?"

"My ex said so," she replied as if insulted.

"Why would there be rival Colombians?"

"It's all business, Mr. Detective. Who can move the most weight. It was the guy from Brooklyn or Hugh. Hugh was the real mover, so these Colombians would come to him to make deals. Hugh played one against the other to get the best deal, and then sold his shit at top dollar to his clientele."

"So, there is another group of Colombians selling shit?"

She nodded. "There are at least two."

The two Wall Street executives sat in the exclusive restaurant with plates of designer food in front of them—meaning miniscule portions elaborately laid out on a plate. The executive on the right was sandy-haired and reasonably handsome, dressed in a crisp shirt and tie. His colleague, who sat next to him, was dark-haired, pudgy and already into his third glass of scotch on the rocks.

"There were these Colombians at the parties," the sandy-haired one said.

David sat across from them, a vodka tonic within reach. "Why is he drinking so much?" David gestured with his chin to his pudgy companion.

"Look, mister," Pudgy replied, "I'm a married man. I can't afford this getting out."

David nodded. "Mum's the word, chief. But that's only if you cooperate."

"Well," Pudgy began, visibly uncomfortable, "Collin here is right; there were these very tough dudes there who were rumored to be Colombians. Nobody really knew for sure. They wouldn't participate in anything. They just floated around, watching over things."

David sat back in his seat, sipping his scotch. "Probably watching consumption."

"And consumption was high," Collin replied.

"So you guys were mad consumers too?"

"You can say that."

"Yes," Pudgy added. "Yes, we were."

"Did either of you get a chance to talk to any of these Colombians?"

They both shook their heads no.

"So you don't know shit from Shinola, basically. What I want to know is, if there was so much consumption, so much drug dealing, so much prostitution, how was it that the Midnight never got busted by the cops?"

Pudgy was the first to answer. "Word was that the cops were paid off."

"They had to have been," David said, biting his lip then taking another sip. "That's the problem. These Colombians you're talking about were probably cops. Did you ever think of that?"

Both men looked at each other.

"Two rival sets of Colombians under the same roof, at the same party. Well, that would just be asking for trouble—oil and water," David pointed out.

"So you think that these men were cops?" Collin asked.

David nodded. "Looking after their interests."

"That would explain much," Pudgy said.

"Yes, it would," David agreed.

The trio—Margaret, Kevin and David—was in Madison Square Park. The day was sunny and warm. Joggers, dog walkers, and people just taking a stroll—the city was alive around them and bustling with activity.

Kevin sat on a bench with Margaret leaning against him, her head on his shoulder. He had his left arm draped across her back. David paced back and forth in front of them tensely, his hands in his jeans pockets, staring down at the ground.

"So you think they were cops?" Kevin asked.

"Makes sense. Protecting their investment, making sure it wasn't going south," David said.

"So the cops are in deep with this?"

"I even think it's possible that Chase's bust was because of a tip from Hugh Osterman to his cop friends. That way Chase would lose his shit."

"That doesn't make sense," Margaret replied. "With the way you two talk about how his connections were on his ass, he should have known interfering with Chase's delivery would impact his business. That would be like cutting off your nose to spite your face."

"Not true," Kevin put in. "Osterman probably thought that the Colombians would deal with him directly, and therefore have another shipment sent to him to cover demand. When the Colombians short-changed him, he was stuck."

"Stuck deep. These cokeheads can be pretty insistent," David said.

"So, what's next for the super sleuths?" Margaret asked, running her hand down the front of Kevin's thin sweater.

David stopped pacing, and then started working on a rock embedded in the dirt with the toe of his shoe. "I wonder why MacDonald didn't say anything in the interview about the cops being present. He should have told us that there were cops in the Midnight for protection—making sure the dealers were selling and not using."

"Maybe," Kevin ventured, "he didn't want to drop a dime on his cop friends. Maybe he was frightened."

"Maybe. That would have helped us a lot," David said, his eye caught by a shapely girl on a bike riding nearby.

Margaret sat up. "That would also explain how the killer got past the gate and simply walked into the house. He could have been flashing a badge."

"That makes some sense," Kevin said. "And certainly cops can kill."

"They make the best assassins, don't they?" David quipped.

"So now this is a cop hunt?" Kevin asked.

"I would rather it end here, guys," Margaret said.

David approached the two and stood over them. "The question is now how to hunt the most dangerous thing in New York. Crossing the thin blue line is not going to be fun or easy."

"Fun?" Margaret said. "It's downright fucking dangerous."

"We can't go to Ferryman and Reynolds," Kevin said, nervously running his fingers through his hair, and retrieving his arm from around Margaret as he sat up. "They'll only go on the defensive. And if the case starts turning in that direction, they'll only deflect it."

David moved away from his friends, since he suddenly surrounded by a group of small yapping dogs on leashes as their owner walked by. "I hate dogs," he said with obvious distaste.

"Why?" Margaret said with a pout. "They are *so* cute."

"They jump up on your pants with their dirty paws, and then their owners act like they're people, telling them to get offa you, instead of yanking on their leashes. I'm sick of that shit."

"Well, we all have to live together in peace," Margaret said firmly, as if that settled the matter.

Kevin stood from the bench and addressed David. "Any ideas?"

"Lean hard on MacDonald?" David asked.

"No, I don't think he'll react well to the casual lean. We have to think of something else."

"The third man out in Osterman's little crew is Two Smooth," David said. "I'll go brace him tonight, and this time you stay gone."

"My pleasure," Kevin smirked.

"And what will you do?"

"I'll keep going down the list, interviewing the names in the cell phone

Records—"

"Do you think that's safe, Kevin?" Margaret said from behind him, still sitting on the bench. "I mean, *by yourself.*"

"It'll be safe," Kevin sighed.

"I think this investigation is going over the thin blue line, buddy. Are you ready for that?" David asked.

"If you are."

David nodded sternly. "I'm going to take off and get some lunch. Tonight, visit Two Smooth. I'll need the car."

"Keys on the bookshelf, buddy," Kevin said. "I'll see you in the morning."

"Yeah, in the morning."

As he followed the young man from Two Smooth's entourage who was serving as his guide, David looked around the room at the décor. It was very simple, with a touch of eighties style to it. Basketball knick-knacks on the mantelpiece, comfortable chairs and couches, a large, widescreen TV showing a basketball game. Sitting in the chairs nearest the TV were a group of boisterous young black men. When some heavy action hit the game, they jumped up and down, shouting and high-fiving each other.

They walked on, past a dining area, where David glimpsed a group of women in bikinis chatting at a large round table, their conversation as heated as the shouts from the basketball game.

David continued to follow his guide until they reached the glass doors of the patio. The floodlights outside the house pushed back the gloom of the night to reveal a sizable patio paved with red octagonal brickwork. Atop it were comfortable lounge chairs, deck chairs, and tables. Two Smooth Williams' skinny pale white body was clearly visible, stretched out on one of the lounge chairs. He was smoking a cigar, while a pretty bikini-clad Latina lay entwined with him.

"Detective," he said in a friendly voice, "make yourself a drink. Get comfortable."

"Thanks." David crossed over to a rolling minibar and poured himself a tall scotch on the rocks. He learned long ago that the trick is to always have something in your hand in case you need to use it as a weapon. It wasn't such a bad idea to be fortified with a couple of strong belts of scotch too.

"So," Two Smooth began, smiling a wide gold-plated smile. "What brings you to my crib?"

"You had cops at the Midnight?" David asked as he pulled over a lounge chair and sat on its edge, facing Two Smooth and his woman.

Two Smooth thought that over for a moment. "Oh, you found out?"

"Yeah."

"So? A lot of places use off-duty cops as security."

"No, they don't," David said, turning the glass up to his face. "Retired and ex – cops, yeah. But these were probably off-duty cops, like you said. How much did you have to pay them to allow you guys to deal?"

Two Smooth sighed, and then remained silent.

"You sure you want her here?" David asked, nodding at the half-naked Latina.

"She's cool, my dude," Two Smooth said.

"Yeah, okay," David went on. "So you had these off-duty police-men protecting their own operation."

"Well, it wasn't *their* operation," Two Smooth said. "Although Blanchard would have liked to think so. They are not a bad group of cops. Because they're still cops, they don't press us too hard. They work *with* us, you know what I mean?"

"Yeah, you scratch their backs, they scratch yours, right?"

"You got it. They were there for protection, and to make sure we were selling shit and not using it—to be sure we were making a profit."

"And by the looks of it, you guys had a very profitable business."

"You can say that," Two Smooth puffed on his cigar.

"Blanchard, who's Blanchard?"

"Sylvester Blanchard. He's the lieutenant that busted the place first. Him and another cop—" Two Smooth's brow furrowed while he thought of the name. "Derek Heidelman! Yeah, they both came into the office one night, asking to speak to the top dog. Hugh and I were the only ones in there, counting cash. They read the charges against us, and then asked if we wanted them to go away. We knew it was a shakedown, so we asked how much."

"How much?"

"Two hundred thou a week."

David whistled. "You dogs are really high rolling."

"So are those cops, my dude." Two Smooth took another puff. "Then, they started poppin' in at the club, snooping around, just chillin' there. They were beginning to freak out the regulars, so we made up this Colombians story. You know, like they were Juan Valdez checking up on his coffee."

"And your patrons thinking they were Colombians, it calmed them down?"

"Better than telling them cops were about in their party would."

David thought for a moment as he took a healthy sip from his glass. "How many cops would you say?"

"Five."

"Would you give me *their* names, or do I have to find that out on my own, too?"

"You're good," Two Smooth said with his signature gold-plated smile. "Faster than an ordinary cop. They haven't put the pieces to-gether yet. Yeah, I'll give you the names because you'll only be back here repeating them to me later, my dude. And I don't want you to put me down as uncooperatin'."

"Thanks. Let me ask: so none of the cops who interviewed you asked about the Colombians?"

"No."

David finished his drink, stood up and went over to the minibar to rest his glass. "Thanks for the information, Two Smooth."

"Don't mention it. Wait a sec, I'll be right back." Two Smooth slipped out from under his woman and headed inside. He returned with a pad and pen, and started writing something. Then he tore the paper free and handed it to David. "Here."

David was in the process of turning off his IC recorder when he looked up and took the paper. He did a quick scan of the contents and then asked, "Is this all of them?"

"Look for yourself."

David read it again. "Two Smooth, I can't tell you what a pleasure it is dealing with you."

"Chill, bro'."

THE WAR WITHIN

Jefferies sat on the edge of the desk in his office, loosened his tie and unbuttoned his collar.

"Yeah, I suspected that," he said. "I had heard rumors and oblique reports about the Midnight. Some said that it was being squeezed by officers from the 51st. And when I heard that Osterman was one of the managers of the club, well, I was sure we had an I.A.B. situation brewing. But before I put I.A.B. on it, I wanted to put my outsider on it. So now you have documented proof?"

Kevin, who sat on the couch against the wall, nodded. "You know we keep transcripts and reports on everything. You'll have enough documentary evidence for a prosecution when we're done."

"That's what I like to hear."

"So, are you going to I.A.B. about these cops?"

"Right now you guys just got rumors and finger-pointing," Jefferies said.

"You had the same information? Rumors and finger-pointing?"

"Rumors—no finger-pointing. In a precinct, everyone knows what everyone else is up to, most of the time. It's like a family of sorts."

"Yeah, I know all about it, Sam."

"Well, then you know I couldn't trust Ferryman and Reynolds on this case. You can see they haven't even caught up with your information yet."

"Well, it might not be their fault." Kevin sat back in his chair.

"People are normally distrustful of the badge and the gun. When you approach them with an ID that says PRIVATE detective and a badge, and tell them you're a private dick, well, that's a different story."

"They're more cooperative, I'm sure."

"Yes."

Jefferies grew thoughtful for a few minutes, and then said, "I don't want you giving reports to Reynolds and Ferryman for a while. I don't want them getting wind of this possible corruption in the department."

"Why? Do you think they'll warn them?"

"No, I don't think so; but the fewer people that know about this before the I.A.B., the better."

"Sure, whatever you want, Sam."

"Kevin," Jefferies asked, "how have you been sleeping?"

Kevin frowned. "Good, why?"

"You've got dark circles around your eyes. And you appear to have lost some weight."

"I'm fine, boss. I sleep like a rock."

"I gave Dr. Fagen your new address. I felt you needed to see him."

"Yeah, he and David had a pretty bad altercation. David ran him out of the apartment."

"David did, huh?"

"Yeah, when I saw David afterward, he was really livid."

Jefferies sat there, staring. "You've been taking your medication?"

"What is this, Sam? What's going on?"

"Nothing, Kevin. It's just that—" Jefferies slid off the top of his desk and crossed the room, taking a seat on the opposite end of the couch from Kevin. "You look like the case is wearing you down. I don't want you to become ill because of it."

"You're just worried because I froze up when I was with David in Chase Arthur's apartment, aren't you?"

Jefferies sighed. "It's that and more, buddy. I don't think the two of you should go together to these dangerous places. You believe there are two of you there, when there's really only one."

"Are you saying I'm that useless? That I can't be counted on?" Kevin asked with a slightly hurt and bewildered expression on his face.

"I'm only saying that David is more skilled at handling dangerous situations, while you are the more cerebral, investigatory half of the team. David, being ex-military and all, is better suited to the physically challenging aspects of the case."

Kevin stood up to signal his intention to leave. "I came to give you our reports and transcripts for the week, Sam. I'm heading home."

"You should drop by Dr. Fagen's office. You should be talking to him."

"I need to be talking to some suspects, Sam—I need to be full-bore on this investigation," Kevin countered.

"Whatever you say, Kevin," said the captain in a resigned tone of voice.

When Kevin got home, he tossed his keys on the bookshelf and crossed the room to the john. He took a piss, leaving the door open.

A few seconds later, David emerged from his room clad only in his pajama bottoms. When he saw Kevin standing over the bowl, he said, sounding totally disgusted, "Dude, why don't you ever close the door?"

"Why? *You* never do."

"I need you to beat feet, yo'. I have Mary in the bedroom."

"You brought that snow bunny back in here?"

"Shit, yeah. Snow bunnies are incredible. They're like fucking porn stars."

"I can imagine." Kevin went into his room and started picking up shirts from the floor, sniffing at the armpits, then tossing them aside.

"Kevin," David said to his back.

"I know, I know. I just want a fresh shirt."

"You call those *fresh*?"

Kevin stopped in the midst of his endeavor, looked at David, and then resumed as he said flatly, "I spoke to Jefferies today."

"And?"

Kevin related the main points of the conversation he'd had with Jefferies while he found a shirt that didn't smell and started to change into. "What are we going to—"

"David!" Mary called from the other room. The conversation stopped as she appeared in front of them naked on her way into the bathroom. "Comin' back to bed?" she asked David coyly as she passed by.

"Yeah. In a minute," David said.

Kevin, now dressed, headed for the living room. "So, what's next with you?"

"I'm going to brace this Blanchard guy," David said. "See what he can tell me about his side dealings. Where are you going?"

"I'm spending the night at Margaret's, then I'm going to see Dr. Fagen in the morning."

"You going to see that quack?"

"Yeah, he's kind of like a friend."

"Don't let him play that cell phone trick on you."

"Yeah. I'll see you tomorrow sometime."

"Sure."

Kevin grabbed his keys and was out the door.

David returned to the bedroom. A second later, Mary came running through the door and dove into the bed, kicking at the sheets playfully with her feet. David jumped in with her, grabbed her, stilled her and held her close.

"Hey, baby," he began.

"Yeah?"

"So, what do you think of black men?"

She looked up at him, staring directly into his eyes. "I find them interesting," she said, frowning. "Why do you ask?"

"I just wanna know, that's all."

Mary nestled her body up against his. "You're silly."

"Yeah, but I've got balls, right?"

She laughed. "You want to shut up and use them?"

He kissed her.

Kevin headed over to the parking garage of the building where Dr. Fagen had his office, his left arm resting comfortably outside the window, whistling all the way. Unlike David, he felt no animosity toward the good doctor, and was actually looking forward to speaking with him, if only because he had something specific on his mind. When, about a month ago, Kevin decided that Fagen was becoming a nuisance, he suggested to David that they move without telling him their whereabouts. Now that Fagen knew where they lived, and he was once again becoming an annoyance, Kevin planned to tell him to leave them alone—once and for all.

Kevin arrived at Fagen's office and entered his sparsely decorated waiting room. Since the doctor had no receptionist and the door to the consulting room was closed, Kevin sat down to wait. A few minutes later, the door opened, and a tall brunette beauty emerged with Fagen close behind her. She thanked him, nodded at Kevin, and left.

When the doctor spotted Kevin waiting for him, he exclaimed, "Kevin! What a surprise! Come in, come in." As Kevin passed him on his way into the consulting room, Fagen patted him lightly on the back and said, "It's so good to see you, my boy." The doctor closed the door behind them and headed for his desk.

Kevin took a seat in the chair facing him and said, "Good to see you too, doc."

"Does David know you're here?"

"Yes."

"How does he feel about that?"

"He calls you a quack."

"Why didn't I guess that?" the doctor replied, rhetorically.

"I'm not here for a session, doc," Kevin said as he shifted uncomfortably in the high-backed leather chair. "I just wanted to tell you to ease up on us this time."

"Ease up?"

"Yeah. Don't pester the shit out of us like you did before."

"Oh, no," the doctor said as he leaned back in his chair. "I don't intend to pester you, Kevin. I'm only here to help you."

"You always say that."

"And I mean it. How have you been sleeping?"

"Good, doc."

"Do you sleep soundly for long periods of time?"

"Sleep like the dead, almost like forever," Kevin deadpanned, venting some of his antagonism with an over-the-top response.

"With all of the sleep you're getting, can you explain the dark circles under your eyes?" The doctor reached for a pen and some paper, evidently poised to make some notes.

"I've been working hard on this damn case."

"How about your medications? Have you been taking them regularly?"

"No."

"Why not?"

"Because I don't hear voices anymore, doc."

"Do you see people?"

"No."

"Ever want to kill yourself?"

"No," Kevin said flatly, while squirming in his seat. "What the fuck is this about, doc?"

The doctor replied, "Just a few innocent questions. That's all."

Kevin sat brooding for a moment. "Show me that cell phone trick you did for David that freaked him out so," he said.

The doctor smiled. "I'm sorry, it won't work now."

"Why?"

"The circumstances are different."

"Smoke and mirrors, that's all it is, smoke and mirrors."

"You could say it's something like that."

Kevin stood up to leave. "Well, I think I said hello, doc. So now it's goodbye."

Fagen also stood up and said rather haltingly, "I understand. But… hmm… Kevin?"

"Yeah, doc?"

"Could both you *and* David come to my office and speak with me? Or maybe I can come over and speak with the two of you."

"I'll ask David," Kevin said as he walked to the door. "You have a beautiful day, doc."

"You too, Kevin, and thanks for stopping by."

After picking up an armload of transcripts from One Police Plaza, David headed to the 51st precinct, an old building that almost looked like a fortress. The central hallway was quiet, with a few individuals sitting on benches that lined the walls. As David approached the tall front desk, the two cops sitting behind stared down at him. One was dark-haired, with a muscular build that was evident despite his uniform.

"How can I help you?" he asked.

"I'm looking for Lieutenant Sylvester Blanchard," David replied firmly.

"What's your name?"

"Detective David Allerton."

"Okay, have a seat Mr. Allerton." The same officer motioned with his head to the benches.

David took a seat, and shortly thereafter an officer emerged from a side door and approached him. "Mr. Allerton, follow me."

"Yeah." David stood and followed the officer through a maze of hallways, passing scores of uniformed officers, to finally arrive at a steep winding staircase. After climbing several flights of stairs to the third floor, he followed his guide through a large office area studded with low cubicles until they reached the door to one of several windowed offices that bordered the open space. The officer took hold of the knob, swung the door open, and stepped out of the way for David to enter.

Inside, David faced a room cluttered with stacks of paperwork almost everywhere. Numerous framed photographs sat atop a credenza along the back wall, underneath the window sill, while a sizable desk occupied the left side of the room. He was surprised to see that the desk before him was rather neat, with only one tidy pile of papers on its surface.

From behind the desk rose a husky well-built man, growing paunchy at the waistline. His hair was dark and graying, and despite the lines and crevices in his face, he was still quite handsome; he sported a mustache that made him look rather distinguished.

He wore a dark blue pinstripe suit with a white shirt, a navy blue tie and gold cufflinks that flashed when he extended his hand to David.

"Detective Allerton, how can I help you?" he asked as the two shook hands.

"Mind if I have a seat?" David motioned to a sofa against the wall.

"Yeah, sure, cop a squat." Blanchard sat down in his chair, which squeaked when he landed. "What's up?"

"I have a few questions concerning a case I'm working on, and I thought you could give me a little insight."

"Yeah, go ahead."

David held up the IC recorder. "Mind if I record this?"

Blanchard sat back and crossed his arms over his chest. "No—go right ahead."

"Thanks," David said as he turned on the device. "I'm investigating the murder of Hugh Osterman in upstate New York—"

"A little outside of everyone's jurisdiction down here, don't you think?"

"The investigation led us down here—"

"What do you mean, *led*?"

"Well, it appears that Mr. Osterman, along with his partners, ran a club called the Midnight, downtown."

"Yeah, and what has that got to do with me?"

David's face darkened with consternation as he replied, "I'm an investigator, Lieutenant. The case has led me to you."

"In what way, Detective?" Blanchard never strayed from his poker face.

"You and some of the boys in your division were shaking down the managers of the Midnight, weren't you?"

Blanchard feigned a smile as he said, flatly, "I'm sorry. I don't know what you're talking about."

"I have firsthand accounts from *several* people that you were the muscle for the club, and also took a pretty hefty payoff to look the other way."

"I can assure you I'm being falsely accused. This information must be coming from my enemies in the area trying to pin some shit on me."

"Is that a fact?" David asked, trying not very hard to hide the sarcasm in his voice.

"Yeah. I don't know the owners of the Midnight, other than what I've read in the reports."

"So you're telling me that you haven't been receiving two-hundred thousand dollars a week from the owners?"

"I'm telling you. Nada," he added with a grin.

"You don't know of a thug named Two Smooth Williams?"

"Nope."

"A drug dealer named Chase Arthur?"

"I know of him only from the police reports."

"Stewart MacDonald?"

"Reports."

"Pamela Walker?"

"Murder victim."

"So you have no idea, no clue, no knowledge whatsoever of any corruption in your precinct?"

"Nope."

David nodded sternly. "I see. Well, could you be of any help to me at all concerning this case?"

"Not really. I can only read back to you what's in the reports." Blanchard cracked a smug smile from the corner of his mouth.

"Of course you know that I have to report everything that I've got on this case to I.A., correct?"

"You got to do what you got to do, Detective."

David stood up from the couch. "We're on the same side, Lieutenant. We're all just trying to solve this case."

"Meaning?"

"Meaning a little cooperation can go a long way."

Blanchard sat forward in his seat, which creaked again, rested his elbows on the desk and growled, "You come into my office and accuse me and my division of shaking down local clubs, and you want fucking cooperation?"

"I'm just telling you about some of the evidence we're getting from people we've interviewed in the course of our investigation. I'm giving you a chance to represent yourself. To give your side of the story."

"I gave you my side of the story, Detective." Blanchard's face was starting to turn red with his vehemence. "I don't know what you're talking about, and my impression is that my foes are trying to railroad me. Consider carefully the nature of the sources of your information."

"I'll do that."

"Grand, just grand. Now. I have work to do, Detective. Real work," Blanchard said by way of a dismissal.

David went to the glass door, its shades rustling as he took hold of the knob. "Blanchard. Do you know of anyone willing to, or capable of, killing Osterman?"

"The list is too long, Detective."

"Give me the top of your list, then."

"Me."

"You're goddamn right he would," Derek Heidelman said, sitting in Katz's Delicatessen with a huge pastrami sandwich before him. "Blanchard would bust a cap in his mother if pressed."

Heidelman was tall, with the long arms and athletic build of a basketball player; he had dark hair and darker eyes. He hefted his sandwich in both hands and took a big bite. Despite the mouthful of food, he managed to say, "But that's why he's a lieutenant and we're the stooges."

"When you say *we*, you mean—?" Kevin asked. He had a simple turkey ham and cheese sandwich on his plate, so far unmolested.

"DeShawn Greene, Karl Montgomery, and Shah Isharri. We were all helping Blanchard out. I never really saw any official shakedown, you know." He stopped chewing and swallowed hard. "This cooperation goes on my record, right?"

"Yes, it does, Derek."

He nodded, more confident now. "I never saw any official misconduct—I just want to make that clear. At best, we were doing some night crawling in a local club. I never had to provide muscle."

"But you were witness to rampant drug use as well as prostitution."

"Look, there are a lot of times when you see things you aren't supposed to act on. Our superior officer said it was cool. If he says it flies, it flies."

"I see."

"I'm clean, chief."

"Well, did you even know Hugh Osterman?"

"No. I saw him a couple of times in the club, but that was it. We weren't pals or anything like that."

"And how much did you get paid doing this so-called night crawling?"

"Well—" Heidelman faltered as he toyed with the sandwich in his hand. "We got ten thousand a night."

"Not very shabby to hang around and do nothing all night. You didn't feel the slightest bit guilty?"

"Hey, they were paying and they made up the numbers. All I did was show up."

Kevin nodded. "So, earlier you said that Blanchard would have the moxie to kill Osterman, right?"

"Yep," he said while he chewed another mouthful.

"Why do you say that?"

Heidelman swallowed before he answered. "They were having a nasty fight as of late. Something about Osterman not having the money to pay Blanchard because of an accounting error."

"Oh, that's what they were calling it, huh?"

"You mean it wasn't? They were lying?" Heidelman seemed genuinely surprised.

"No, they ran into money problems alright, but it wasn't because of some accounting error. But go on… they were fighting?"

"Yeah, Blanchard didn't want to hear that shit, he wanted his money. He told Osterman that too—not to fuck with him or he'd be sorry in the morning."

"Was this the night before the murder?"

"Naaah," Heidelman shook his head. "That's what Blanchard likes to say. Everything 'in the morning.' 'I'll do it, but I'll hate myself in the morning,' shit like that."

"Figure of speech," Kevin clarified.

"Yeah, so they had it out a couple of times, especially when they started counting money upstairs. Everybody was getting edgy at the club. You could see it in the patrons. They were looking less like partygoers and more like fried-out zombies."

"Supply was drying up."

"Less people were showing up at the club, so less money all around. Osterman tried to convince Blanchard of this over and over again, but Blanchard kept the lean on him."

"Let me ask you. Do you think Blanchard could have given the order to one of his men to kill Osterman?"

Heidelman shook his head. "No. Blanchard is a mean cuss, like I said; he'd pop his own mother. I can see Blanchard doing something like that all on his own—completely solo."

***

"I think we got our man," Kevin said, flipping through the transcript from David's interview with Blanchard. "He's lying through his teeth."

"Yeah, but you don't have anyone telling us that Blanchard ordered the hit." David went to the refrigerator, pulled out a carton of milk and drank from the carton.

"No, he would most likely do that himself." Kevin tossed the transcript on the growing stacks of documents on the table.

"So, what we need is the murder weapon," David said. "That's the only thing that would place Blanchard in the same space and time as Osterman on his last day on earth."

"And how are we going to get it? Ask him for it?" Kevin said. "It's not his service revolver because you can't put a silencer on those."

"No, it has to be at home, locked away."

"Like I said, what are you going to do, ask him for—" Kevin suddenly sat straight up in the kitchen chair, and said with some alarm, "Don't tell me you're thinking about breaking into a cop's home."

"Like you said, what am I going to do, ask him for the gun?" David countered.

"You know this man will kill you if he finds you in his home."

"Don't worry, I'm good at this. If I find a gun that passes ballistics and is registered to him, the game is over."

"I think you're crazy," Kevin said, half-heartedly.

"I think it'll work. I just need you to be the lookout."

Shaking his head in frustration, Kevin persisted. "Yeah, sure, but tell me, why don't we just go to Jefferies and ask him to get a search warrant, and we'll search his home for the weapon that way? You know—the legal way?"

"Have you ever tried to get a search warrant on a cop? They always find out. Give this man a minute and he'll make the gun disappear. He's not stupid. He knows that the gun connects him to the murder, so he's not going to be caught with it so easily," said David.

"So you plan to just go in and steal it?"

"Yeah," David replied cockily. "If it passes as our murder weapon, and it's registered to that scumbag, I'll hand it over to Jefferies."

"Slick. When are you going to do this?"

"I'm going to stake out his home this week. Are you game?"

Night had already fallen on the sleepy residential street in Queens. The sour lemon eye of the moon hovered overhead, wavering behind heavy slow-moving clouds. Kevin was bent over in the passenger seat, asleep. David, who was leaning up against the driver's-side door, was staring fixedly at the Blanchard home, just across the street. At one point, a group of teenagers left the house, rushed an old Nissan Sentra in the driveway, backed it up and drove off. A large, black Escalade was left behind.

Soon after, around seven, Sylvester Blanchard and his wife emerged from their home, climbed into the Escalade and took off down the street. David picked up a pair of binoculars from the dashboard and scanned the windows, finding no sign of life in any of the rooms. He tapped Kevin on the shoulder with the binoculars, and he awoke with a start.

"It's time," David said. He dropped the binoculars in Kevin's lap, leaned over and opened the glove compartment, retrieving black gloves and a black ski mask. "Keep your eyes open. I don't want them sneaking up on my ass."

Kevin yawned heavily. "Yeah."

"I'm serious, Kevin. Don't fuck this up on me."

"I'm watching, I'm watching."

David first donned his gloves, then opened the door and slipped out into the night. Ducking low as he crossed the street, he darted up the Blanchards' driveway and ran alongside the house toward the back where a large garage loomed. David pulled on the ski mask and climbed the flight of stairs that led to the back door. He took out his lock pick set, produced a well-worn credit card and jiggled it between the bolt and the strike plate to pop the lock.

He slipped inside, smiling to himself. Just like a cop not to have an alarm system, unless it was one of those silent numbers. Either way, David moved fast. Heading directly upstairs to the largest bedroom in the house he dug around, under the bed and through the closets. He quickly found a lockbox on the upper shelf of one of the closets. Dropping to the floor and using his lock pick set, he easily turned the lock and opened the box, finding two colts inside. A .45 auto and a .38 semi. Jackpot! As he kissed the .38, David heard the front door open and close downstairs.

He stashed the gun into his jacket, closed the lock box, and stood upright to put it back in its place. He closed all the closets and crept stealthily out of the bedroom, crossed the carpeted hall to the top of the stairs and started down to the foyer. But he stopped midway when he saw lights coming on. He could hear one set of footfalls. They were light—a woman most likely. He heard keys strike a table. There was a brief moment of quiet, and then the sound of the woman talking on the phone.

David eased down the stairs, and once at the bottom he peeked down the hall into the kitchen. Mrs. Blanchard was pacing back and forth as she chatted on her cell phone, oblivious to his presence. David stepped across the foyer into the living room, which was still dark. He could hear the front door opening again. This time he ducked behind the heavy curtains at the living room window and froze. These were heavy footfalls, and David could hear Blanchard call out to his wife and then head upstairs.

David opened the window behind him, popped the screen and dropped into the driveway at the side of the house. He dashed across the street to the car and found Kevin sound asleep in the passenger's seat. David yanked open the driver's side door, sat down next to his partner and elbowed him in the ribs to awaken him.

Kevin jumped awake and looked at him groggily. "Wha—?"

"You were supposed to beep me if someone came home, jackass."

David slid into the car, slammed the door shut and then yanked off the ski mask. "You almost fucked things up in there, buddy."

"You did fine. Did you get it?"

"Yeah, I got it." He reached into his jacket and handed the pistol over to Kevin, who looked at it as he held it in both hands. "Wow, you were right. We got the motherfucker."

"No thanks to you." David started up the car.

"What do you mean?" Kevin replied angrily, as he stashed the gun in the glove compartment. "Beeping the horn was idiotic anyway—it only draws attention."

"Bullshit. A horn beeping on the street can be anyone. No one suspects anything from an innocent beeping of a horn," David said as he drove away, leaving the Blanchard house behind, a fading image in the rearview mirror.

A CONFERENCE OF IDIOTS

"It's not the murder weapon," Charles Stafford, head of ballistics, said, dropping a folder on the table. "Nothing matches."

"Not even close, Charlie?" Kevin asked, sitting on the edge of the table. He reached for the folder, studying the photos and the report.

"This gun was never anywhere near Osterman." Stafford returned to his desk across the room, stopped over it, and retrieved another folder. "Where did you get it?"

"I found it hidden somewhere," Kevin said evasively. "When can I have it back?"

"Ten minutes."

"And you're absolutely sure it wasn't the weapon used in the murder?"

"Just as sure as if it was an ice cream cone."

"SHIT!"

"What's the matter? You're behaving as if your entire case hinges on this weapon." Stafford was leaning back against his desk, reading another report. "Does it?"

Kevin bit into the skin of his cracked lower lip. "It kinda does."

"That's too bad." Strafford gestured at Kevin with the folder in his hand. "You have to do a little more police work, that's all. But whoever this weapon belonged to didn't use this one."

"Do me a favor then, Charlie—would you?"

"What's that Kevin? Anything for a good ex-detective."

"Run that gun through your database for me, and see if it matches up with a weapon used in any other murder case. I want to know if there are *any* bodies that connect to it."

"No problem. New York City murders only, with .38-caliber handguns?"

"All over, even New Jersey. How about within an hour's radius by car?"

"Not a problem."

"I already have a stack of reports and transcripts waiting for me in the records room. Can you add that to it after it's ready?"

"No problem."

David drove the Ford Taurus down Second Avenue where the traffic was steady and comprised mostly of taxis. He noticed a black Chrysler two cabs in front of him that kept switching lanes carefully. As it neared Fourteenth Street, its left-hand turn signal began flashing. The two cabs in between pulled out of the turn lane, allowing David to come up slowly behind the Chrysler before it could negotiate the turn.

David considered ducking his head—lest Blanchard notice him in the rearview mirror—but realized that a car seen driving itself would call more attention to itself than one with him sitting behind the wheel. Blanchard soon made the left-hand turn, with David following, leaving a car length between them. They traveled down Fourteenth Street until Blanchard pulled over in front of a row of stores after passing Avenue A.

David drove past him, finding a parking space four cars down. He parked the car and adjusted his passenger-side mirror to watch as Blanchard rounded the front of his car and entered a pet shop. David relaxed in his seat and turned on the radio, scanning the stations for something suitable. In a few seconds, he found some music he liked and sat back to enjoy it. Suddenly, he was disturbed by a metallic tapping against the driver's-side window, and he turned to see a gold shield pressed against it. He rolled down the glass and looked up into the face of a stranger wearing a pair of dark shades.

"Mind stepping out of the car?" the guy with the shield said.

David didn't respond verbally, but instead opened the car door and stepped out into the afternoon sun. Waiting for him were two men in dark suits and shades. The one who ordered him out of the car removed his eyewear to reveal unusually bushy brows. He was a lightly bearded man with a military-style crew cut. He held up his badge again as he identified himself. "Detective Karl Montgomery."

David glanced behind Montgomery to get a better look at his colleague, who was a black man standing behind him. David nodded to Montgomery as he said, "Detective David Allerton."

Montgomery smiled, and then glanced briefly over his shoulder at the officer behind him before replying, "That's funny, I thought you were a cop stalker."

"Very funny," David said. "Can I help you?"

The two police officers stood stock-still.

"Well, Allerton, what's up with you here?" Montgomery asked with a snide smile.

David's features darkened. "Are you guys charging me with anything, like parking at a meter without paying… or something?"

Montgomery looked down at his shoes for a moment, smirking a little, then looked up at David again. "Look, driving around in this neighborhood is dangerous— dangerous to your health. What you need to do is back off. Just because Heidelman is a bitch, doesn't mean the rest of us are."

"Ohhh," David took a step back, nodding in comprehension. "Ohhh, so that's what this is—you're putting me on notice."

"That's right, dumbshit, this is a notice to you and whoever this

Whitehouse dude is, to back the fuck off."

"I'm investigating a murder, and it seems like you're interfering. Should this be a matter for I.A.?"

"We know you aren't with Internal Affairs, so don't try to pull that shit with us. You're not even a cop. You know the saying in this city: 'If you ain't a cop, you'd better not play a cop.' "

"I don't need to play cop here, pal." David's reply was flat and resolute. "And the evidence will speak for itself. I'll have signed affidavits from the individuals who place you guys in the Midnight during the hours when you should've been working."

"How do you know that we weren't?"

"Don't be dense, you're busted—and instead of folding your cards you think you can bluff. Well here's the real deal, smart guy: save your ass jail time and come clean now. This case is not about you and your filthy hands, it's about a murder; and I have reason to believe that one of you performed a hit for someone, and I want names. I want the cop that did it."

The two officers stood rooted to the asphalt for a moment, then Montgomery stepped away to speak in hushed tones to his colleague behind him. David smiled inwardly. They were caving in, but here was the difficult thing: they most likely believed that neither of them was the shooter. Especially if they came clean.

Montgomery walked over to David, his features were tight with concern and some fear. As if he sensed his face revealed too much, he put his sunglasses back on.

"Watch your back, buddy," Montgomery finally said to David.

"That's your reply? That's the best you can come up with?"

"See you in intensive care if you keep it up." And with that, Montgomery turned on his heel and crossed the street with his colleague close behind. With the hole they left in their wake, David suddenly noticed Blanchard standing not too far away. He strolled up to David with his hands in his pockets, whistling a tune.

"You have too many things going against you in this case. You know that, don't you?" Blanchard said, looking relaxed and confident.

"Not enough to keep me from you."

"Just because Heidelman folded doesn't mean shit. It's his word against ours."

"And about two dozen other witnesses."

"There's an explanation for everything. Trust me—you'll find out."

"I'm certain that I will," David shot back.

"Watch out. You're on the shit list of three cops. That's bad news."

David, more thoughtful now, said, "Don't you worry—I'll be careful."

When Blanchard turned around and headed back towards his car, David let out a huge deep breath, and let his shoulders sag as he felt the tension flow out of his body.

"So they leaned on you a little." Kevin was sitting at his laptop, typing away on the keys. "You knew that was going to happen as soon as you crossed the thin blue line."

David was stretched across the couch. "I hate fucking criminal cops. I really do."

"So do I."

"This Montgomery guy—he's a real smooth sweetheart."

"I can imagine that he is," Kevin said as he turned in his seat to face David.

"I want to bust one of those fools. See the look on their faces when they're handcuffed."

"What are we going to do with Blanchard's gun?" Kevin asked as he returned to his typing.

"Mail it to him," David replied.

Kevin stopped typing, and turned once again to face his friend. "Do what?"

"*Mail* it to him."

"You break into the man's house, steal his pistol and then—you *mail* it back?" Kevin sighed in disbelief.

"Third class at that," David added.

"You can't put a gun through the mail."

"The fuck I can't. You think I want to break into his house again with you as a goddamned lookout?"

"You were fine," Kevin reminded him.

"I'm mailing it."

"You're crazy. You're a lunatic."

"You have to be to chase after five cops."

"Blanchard will go ballistic when he opens the package and finds his gun. You know that, don't you?"

"So? You think I give a fuck? He's already drawn the line in the sand," David persisted.

Undaunted, Kevin said, "He's going to know that it's us."

"So?"

"Just so you know what to expect," Kevin explained as he shrugged his shoulders, resigning himself to David's stubbornness—as usual.

"Hmmm, so what do we do now?"

"Phone records?" Kevin suggested.

"Whose?"

Kevin replied as he returned to his typing, "The cops."

"Not without a subpoena."

"Jefferies can get it."

David seemed to ponder this and then said, "I think we need to hand over our reports to Jefferies so he can start filing them with I.A. We might need a little help here. That way Jefferies can get us shit like phone records with no problem."

"I'll start making copies," Kevin offered.

Suddenly looking deflated, David admitted, "I'm telling you one thing, though. I'm running out of ideas."

"Well, let's just say that one of the cops killed Osterman. Why would they do it? Did one become a paid assassin?"

"Money problems?" David said, sitting up on the couch. "Subpoena bank records?"

"Getting paid what they were? I don't think so."

"Unless one of them had a drug habit. Coke will eat through your paycheck no matter how fat it is."

"So, one of the cops has a bad habit. Why don't you ask your dealer friend, Two Smooth?"

"Naaah. He would have told me,"

"So, no dope problems. Then what?"

David, restless now, shifted his position before he answered. "I don't think their bank records will reveal anything. Dirty cops usually bury their ill-gotten gains in their backyard until retirement. If they were hurting for money, it would most likely come from that fund, not their paychecks."

"Not money, not drugs. Revenge?" Kevin suggested.

"For what, a grudge? How do you fuck with a cop?"

"Fuck with his money."

"We may have something there." David said, nodding in agreement. "Osterman was hurting for drugs, maybe he was hurting for money, too."

"Maybe not. They were rolling in cash. I'm sure they had reserves."

"Shit!" David got to his feet and headed to the front door, then turned around to express his growing impatience. "We'll never find the killer this way. Bastard is as good as gone."

"There's only one thing left to do, Dave."

"What?"

Kevin sat back in his wooden desk chair. "Turn up the heat on the cops."

"Get Internal Affairs on their asses," David said while he pointed at Kevin. "Let those fuckers dig in their business for a while. Might get them to act."

"Act?"

"Jump. Flinch. Take a swipe at us, Kev."

"Do we really want them taking a swipe at us? They already threatened you."

"That was bullshit. Trying to rattle our cage," replied David, dismissively.

"So you want to rattle back I suppose."

"*I think that's a really bad idea!*" Margaret shouted from Kevin's bedroom.

Kevin sighed.

David shook his head.

Jefferies shook his head. "You want to get I.A. on this already?" he asked.

Kevin sat on the couch in his office. "Yeah. We want them digging in these guys' personal affairs as soon as possible. We need them off-balance."

Jefferies poured over the paperwork that Kevin had brought, an elbow on the desk, a hand against the side of his head. "You've got a lot of evidence here. They'll act on it alright."

"Do you think we can get our hands on their status reports?"

"I can make that happen," Jefferies assured him.

Kevin stood and smoothed the front of his slacks, more from nerves than creases. "Well, that's what I came for. I'd better get going."

"Kevin?" Jefferies asked without looking up from his desk.

"What?"

"You need to see Dr. Fagen, especially before all this shit comes to a head."

"Why is that, Sam?"

"Your mental stability might come into question."

"Again, Sam—why is that?"

"I think this case is aggravating your condition."

"I don't think so. Could you just get those I.A. boys on these dirty cops for me, please? I'll take care of my mental state."

"If you say so, buddy."

"Thanks a million, Sam."

Kevin was atop Margaret, thrusting into her, while she repeatedly slapped him on the ass, panting: "Go, baby, go." Kevin built up a head of steam, moving faster, hammering deeper—and then stopped. He lowered his body onto her carefully, by leaning on his arms. Margaret blinked in bewilderment, as her turbulent feelings came to an abrupt halt.

"This isn't working," Kevin said, gently rolling off her onto his side of the bed. "I'm sorry, Margie."

Margaret rolled over onto her side, brushing dark strands of hair from her face before placing a hand on his chest. "Are you alright? Something wrong?"

"Jefferies."

"Sam? What about Sam?" Margaret removed her hand and ran her fingers through her long tresses, her body shuddering as it let go of her pent-up passion.

"He said I had to speak to Dr. Fagen," Kevin said, turning his head to face her. "He says that my mental condition is deteriorating."

"He said *that*?"

"Yeah."

There was a pause as each let the implications sink in.

"How do you feel about that?" Margaret asked.

"How do you think I'm *supposed* to feel about that, Margie?"

She was always surprised that Kevin only called her Margie when they were having sex—or right after—and at all other times it was strictly Margaret. She studied his features as he stared up at the ceiling. He was clearly lost in thought.

"Do *you* think you need to see Dr. Fagen?"

"I did already," Kevin said.

"How did that go?"

"It didn't. We didn't have a session."

"Well, that's nothing serious. What did he say?"

"He wanted to see David and I together at a session, but that's going to be impossible because David thinks he's a quack."

Margaret rolled over, and like Kevin, rested on her back while staring up at the ceiling. "You can't let David make decisions for you, Kevin. If you feel that it's important to see Dr. Fagen, I suggest you do that."

Kevin continued to stare at her. "Do you think my mental stability is in question?"

"I don't see anything wrong with you, Kevin."

Kevin smiled. "You're just saying that because you're fucking me."

"I was... I'm not now," Margaret said, coyly.

Kevin rolled over to climb on top of her a second time.

***

David, stark naked, walked around Mary Olman's bed to pick up a teddy bear holding a heart from a nearby chair; he looked at it face to face. Meanwhile, Mary lay on the bed with the blanket pulled up to cover her nude body, and quietly observed David's movements.

"What's the matter, David?"

"Kevin wants to see a shrink."

"So, what has that got to do with you?" Mary asked, puzzled.

"He wants me to go too."

"Why?" she asked, sounding concerned.

David put the teddy bear back on the chair, walked over to Mary's vanity and toyed with the objects he found there.

"People were killed," David said.

"What?"

"*Many* people were killed," David repeated, still trifling with the perfume bottles. "You know, the usual thing: two detectives in a car chase through the city. The perpetrators, in trying to escape, jump a divider and slam into a car in the opposite lane. A family of four is in the other car. Everybody dies when their car explodes into flames. Even the children," David said as he swallowed hard.

"*Oh, my God!*" Mary gasped as she sat bolt upright on the bed.

"Shortly after that, I quit the force. Kevin tried to make it work, but then he was told to enter into treatment with Dr. Fagen—"

"Who is Dr. Fagen?" Mary interrupted.

David finally stepped away from the vanity, and started studying a picture on the wall—standing up close to it and frowning as he scrutinized the tiny faces in the photo. "Our shrink."

"He became yours, too?"

"Dr. Fagen's the reason I ended up moving in with Kevin. He thought it would be better if we lived together, so we could help each other get over the trauma."

"I see," Mary said. "Did that work?"

"We don't talk about it."

Mary nodded without making any comment. She was somewhat dumbfounded—even afraid—of the man now pacing back and forth in her bedroom. David could be dark and moody sometimes. She drew her knees up to her chin—under the blanket—and sighed.

"David, can I ask you a question?" she asked reluctantly.

"What?"

"Well, we've been together for a few days now, and I've never been with a private investigator before. I find it kinda exciting."

"Your point, Mary?"

"I think I'm falling for you."

"But I don't have any coke on me."

She shook her head angrily. "I'm not talking about that, I'm talking about you and me. You're unattached—"

"And I intend to stay that way," David said as he strode across the room and sat down on the side of the bed, near Mary's feet. "Look, you are my little snow bunny," he added, softening. "I don't want to fuck this up with all this love shit. Let's just enjoy ourselves and that way neither of us will get hurt."

"You're just saying that because you don't believe I'll stop tricking for coke."

"Something like that," he admitted.

"What if I told you that I will?"

He looked at her face searchingly and pulled the blanket from her body, revealing her nakedness, which aroused him. Then he just took her, unresisting, with her knees on her chest, her back to the headboard.

***

David took a shower and then—over breakfast—had an animated conversation about the handling of crime in New York City with Mary and her roommate Cheryl that detained him longer than he'd realized. He had planned to get an early start, but time seemed to evaporate. When he looked down at his wristwatch, he was so startled by the time that he immediately got to his feet and prepared to leave, but not before saying his goodbyes.

Mary accompanied him to the front door, and as he slipped out into the hallway, she grabbed him by the forearm, turned him around and planted a long, hungry kiss on his lips. He embraced her in return, and then hit the stairs after reassuring her that he'd be back later.

He trotted down the flights of stairs, exited the building and hurried over to the deserted block where he'd parked his car. When he reached the front passenger side, he noticed that he had a flat tire. He cursed at it, and then stepped around to the trunk where he kept his spare. As he passed the rear passenger-side tire, he found it flat also.

David looked behind the car. Could driving over a single broken bottle flatten both tires? He glanced further down the curb, but didn't see any shattered glass. Then he checked the driver's side of the vehicle, and found those tires were also flat.

"These fucking dirty cops are like demented children," he said to himself as he took out his cell phone to call a tow truck.

Margaret, naked, rounded the cluttered kitchen table in Kevin's apartment to reach the refrigerator. When she peered in, she found it crammed with food items haphazardly arranged on the shelves. She felt lucky when she found an unopened, unexpired tub of peach yogurt. After closing the refrigerator door, she retrieved a clean spoon and began eating her breakfast, while standing over the table. She stopped occasionally to flip through the forensic photographs and re-ports—all of which she gave a cursory glance—until she reached the phone records. She put the yogurt down on the counter as she pulled out one sheaf of papers: the phone records belonging to the ex-wife of Hugh Osterman—Deborah Hendricks. Margaret looked them over with interest.

Kevin walked into the kitchen in his boxers. "You'd better get some clothes on before David walks in," he said when he noticed Margaret was nude.

"Where is David, anyway?"

"God only knows." Kevin crossed the room to where Margaret stood, came up behind her and wrapped his arms around her waist. He buried his face in her neck for a moment, inhaling deeply, then looked over her shoulder and down at the phone records she held in her hands.

"Deborah Hendricks?!" he exclaimed.

"I'm just looking at the wife angle," she said. "I'm looking for a pattern."

"Pattern?"

"Yeah, who is she calling the most?"

"That's easy—Stewart MacDonald."

Margaret unlocked Kevin's arms and turned to face him, cocking her head to one side as if to challenge him. "You know this, how?"

"Because we've reviewed everything here," he said, pointing at the table as he let her go, then picking up her yogurt and spooning it quickly into his mouth.

"You don't find that suspicious?"

"Not really. She was friends with Stewart. She may have gotten her coke from him, or maybe they were lovers. It doesn't make them killers. Besides, the second most called number is Osterman himself. That doesn't mean that there was anything between them other than business."

"I don't think it's my place to talk about a murder investigation, but have you ever thought of the rival angle?" Margaret asked.

"What's that?"

"Maybe one of Pamela Walker's running buddies became her rival. Such as that Francis girl—" Margaret started snapping her fingers in her frustration as she tried to remember her first name.

"Karen Francis?"

"That's her!" Margaret pointed at him. "What if she wanted Osterman's attention? What if she had Pamela Walker bumped off because she wanted to be in her place?"

"So she bumped off Osterman too?" Kevin said as he scraped the bottom of the yogurt carton with his spoon. "Now that seems like a real stretch. Why kill Osterman too?"

"Osterman walked in on the hit and got bumped off for seeing the killer."

"Walked in on them from his lounge chair floating in the middle of his pool?" Kevin held the tub of yogurt over his head like a basketball, and tossed it across the kitchen to the corner where the open garbage pail sat. It struck the rim and fell to the floor.

Margaret sighed audibly before strolling over to the empty container and tossing it in the trash. "Then, who do you think killed Osterman?"

"A cop."

"Just like that?"

"Just like that." Kevin bent over the table, scanning the piles of paper. "A cop was the triggerman. The murder was too clean, too professional to be otherwise."

"What's so professional about walking into a house and knocking off three people. Especially if you know the killer."

"A cop was the triggerman."

"Who was the person *behind* the triggerman, Kevin? That's who you want."

"We find the triggerman, we find the rest of the people involved."

"Cops don't talk, Kevin."

"Yes, they do, Margaret."

"You're going to get yourself killed messing around with the Men in Blue. They have too much to lose."

"It's not my fault they got their balls caught in the wringer."

"And you're turning the crank?" she said, archly.

"And why not?" Kevin persisted.

Shaking her head regretfully, Margaret said, "I hate to say this because I love them so much, but you're going to get your balls shot off messing with five crooked killer cops."

"You love my balls?" he responded, looking surprised.

With a deep sigh, she turned around to peer out the window at the morning streetscape. "You're going to get yourself killed."

Kevin stroked Margaret's hair, pulled the tresses over her ear away and blew into it. Margaret flinched, bringing her shoulder to her ear and laughed. He wrapped his arms around her waist again and gave her a gentle kiss.

"Never mind that—let's just go back to bed," Kevin said with a smile.

"What?" David asked, standing in Jefferies office, while the captain sat behind his desk. "You can't be serious."

"That's what the deposition says," Jefferies stated flatly. He held up a fistful of papers and read from one: "They were on an undercover sting operation."

"Undercover sting—" David muttered in disbelief, as he started to pace in front of Jefferies' desk.

"Not only that, they have proof of their success. They recently snagged for their precinct one of the largest drug shipments ever. That means they stopped a big shipment from coming into the city, so their efforts seem to be paying off. I don't have to tell you that they get a lot of brownie points for that."

"So they're writing all this off? All the bribes to look the other way?"

"Well," Jefferies sighed, as he continued patiently, "they're claiming you and Kevin are spearheading a smear campaign intended to discredit them—to have them removed from the premises *and* the sting operation."

"You can't possibly believe this, Sam." David stopped short, turning back toward Jefferies now. "This is all bullshit."

"I know it's bullshit, David, but this is what I.A. has to work with."

"I have a confession from one of their own men."

"They say he's covering his ass by selling out his friends on this phony story." Jefferies gathered up the material into a nice even pile, shoved them into a manila envelope, and held them out for David.

David stared at the envelope, as if he was not going to claim it. Then, apparently changing his mind, he reached over the desk and took it after all. "This is just a waste of time. We've got to move on these guys, Sam."

"And just how do you think you're going to do that? You have four cops and one fink. Lean on the fink," countered Jefferies.

David thought about it. "Press the fink? Why the fuck would he help me out?"

"His name is shit. No one is going to trust him as a partner. If he's in on the dirty dealing, he's long gone now. He's a man without a country. He might need a friend," Jefferies suggested.

"I don't make friends out of finks. Plus he was covering his own ass. He gave up no kind of fucking evidence. No shooter, no names—he didn't even point a finger at Blanchard."

"Did you really expect him to?" Jefferies got to his feet, pushed his chair back and came out from behind the desk. "He's no fool."

"I'm not leaning on him. Maybe Kevin will blow in his ear. I want Blanchard," David said.

"I'm not too sure you should lean on him now, anyway. He's got that winning streak going on. He's got Captain Mo on his side."

"Captain Mo?"

"Momentum." Jefferies walked over to a small four-cup coffee-maker that sat on a nearby filing cabinet. He took the carafe by the handle and held it up for David to see. "Some oil for your bloodstream?"

David struck his leg with his envelope. "I've got to get moving. I'm going after this motherfucker. He doesn't know what it's going to be like having David Allerton up his ass."

"David Allerton better watch his step. Harassment charges can be brought against private investigators too."

As David walked to the door, he said, "Yeah, as well as assault."

"That's not funny," Jefferies said to the closing door.

"I don't think the killer is so professional," Margaret said, fully dressed now, walking around in her stocking feet with a cup of coffee in her hand.

"I don't think so, either." David was sitting on the couch, his feet cocked up on the coffee table.

"I still think it was a professional hit," Kevin remarked, sitting in his desk chair, facing out into the room.

David turned to Kevin. "You want to brace Heidelman again?"

"Maybe. You think he'll give up anything new?"

"Well, he *is* running out of friends."

"I think you need to leave him alone," Margaret warned. "You're not getting anything from him."

"Now, how do you know that?" David asked her.

"Because you don't believe he'll talk. If you did, you would—how do you say it?— roll up on him yourself."

David laughed at her use of the urban vernacular.

"It has to have been a cop, David," Kevin said.

"Professional, unprofessional," David said. "Blanchard did the hit. I have that feeling."

"Did you mail him back his gun?" Kevin asked.

Margaret did a double take. "Mail him his what?!"

"Yeah, I dropped it off at the 51st precinct mail post. I'd love to see their faces when and if they trace that shit back to one of their very own."

"You have a cop's gun?" Margaret asked in exasperation. "What in the hell possessed you?"

Kevin gestured to his roommate. "It was David's idea."

"Okay, go ahead and blame me," David replied, stretching out on the couch. "Did he tell you how he fell asleep when he was supposed to be my lookout and—"

"Do we really have to go into all that?" Kevin interrupted. After glaring at David and mouthing the words 'be quiet,' he said, "Well, I guess we can call our plan to shake up the dirty cops a bust."

"Oh, but I did shake Blanchard when I broke into his house and made away with that damn gun," David said, yawning. "I know that much."

Margaret smirked at him. "He's coming here to shoot you both in your asses, David."

"Why is this chickenhead in on our conversations?" David asked Kevin angrily.

"Chickenhead?" Margaret was hot. "If Blanchard doesn't, I will!"

"Whoa, whoa, you two," Kevin interjected, waving his hand for attention. "Look, we're brainstorming here, and every brain that we can call upon is welcome."

"Even if it is a chickenhead brain?" David was relentless.

"This just goes to show that you guys are at a dead end with this investigation, when your dumb partner has to attack me." Margaret sought refuge in the chair across the room and sat down.

There was a pregnant pause. Everyone sat staring off into space for a few minutes, not breaking the silence.

"I've got an idea," Kevin said.

"What?" David and Margaret said in unison, then scowled at each other.

"Get your girlfriend to infiltrate the unit, see if she can get under Blanchard's skin."

David frowned, "Kevin, are you high or something?"

"Well, what else would you have us do?"

"Let's use *your* girlfriend," David said as he pointed to Margaret.

"To do what?" Margaret asked, looking perplexed.

"For target practice," David finished sourly.

Margaret waved at him. "I'm not letting *you* get under *my* skin, Davy."

"Don't call me, Davy."

"Davy."

Suddenly, David sat up on the couch. "We're going in the wrong direction. That's the problem. Something happened. Something went wrong and the deal went kaput. So kaput that Blanchard or one of his men was forced to whack Osterman. The question is: what was it?"

"What was it about the deal that went wrong?" Kevin asked.

"As far as we can tell," Margaret said, "the entire enterprise was a win/win for Blanchard."

"Maybe it's a case of driving a good nail into a bad toe," David said.

"Nail... toe?" Margaret asked.

David continued, "Maybe Blanchard, when he busted Chase's shipment, didn't know just how bad that would hurt Osterman's deal. By Osterman giving up the shipment sure as hell proves that *he* didn't."

"So, Osterman calls his friend Blanchard and gives him a hot tip," Kevin ventured. "Blanchard, not knowing how this bust will affect everything in the long run, acts on it, thinking that he is going to score big with the cop brass."

"Only to find out that now Osterman can't come through with his protection money," David continued the extrapolation. "He reminds Osterman what the money is for, Osterman laughs in his face and pisses him off. Blanchard can't afford to look weak because Osterman has a network of underlings from Stewart MacDonald to Chase Arthur. So he gave Osterman an ultimatum—"

Margaret chimed in. "But that makes Blanchard a dumb sonofabitch. He knows that Osterman's shipment was jacked. He knows it was the truth that the cops came down on the shipment."

David shook his head. "Blanchard probably thought that Osterman was lying about his cash flow. Making it *look* like he took a hit being without his shipment. What moron would zap his own pockets? Osterman was a wheeler-dealer, but he was no moron."

"But he certainly underestimated the Colombians," Kevin said.

"Their holding out on giving Osterman that coke certainly fucked the wheeler-dealer," David said. "I think we've got something here."

Margaret, exasperated, threw up her hands. "Please! *Tell me! What* have you got?!"

Both men remained silent.

"You've got to lean on someone. Someone is not telling you something crucial to the case," Margaret added calmly, and sat back in her chair.

Kevin stood up and said, "The question is who? I've got to review the transcripts again." He headed to the kitchen.

David rose too, grabbed the car keys from the coffee table and headed for the front door. Margaret followed closely behind him.

"David," she said to his back.

He stopped and turned to face her. "What?"

"Look, I know there's bad blood between us, but for Kevin and for the sake of our relationship, can we *please* get past it?"

David sighed. "I don't know what you're talking about, Margaret."

"The constant insults and attacks. I've done nothing to deserve such treatment from you."

This time, David tried to take a softer tone. "Don't take it personal, but you're not a detective. We are professionals here, with a very real murder investigation on our hands, and you are just—someone with some free time and curiosity. But we don't have time for this. Every day the trail gets colder and the killers get further out of reach. Every day he's fucking with you, he's not keeping his nose to the grindstone. Kevin is the brains of this operation, I'm the brawn. Simple as that. If we're stuck, it means that he is preoccupied. Preoccupied with you."

Margaret looked genuinely bewildered and upset. "But he's in there poring over transcripts as we speak, so how can you say that he's preoccupied?"

"Because the minute I walk out this door, you'll be in the kitchen, distracting him."

She thought about that. "Hold on," Margaret said as she approached the couch to grab her sweater. "Kevin!" she called out. "I'm leaving!"

"Awwright!" said Kevin's voice from the kitchen.

"Could you drop me off at home, David?" Margaret asked as she followed him out the door.

David looked at her incredulously. "You're kidding me."

"Like you said, he needs to get to work without any distractions.

So—can I get that lift?"

"I think we can live under the same roof," David said, pulling the car to the curb before he stopped. They were in Brooklyn Heights, on a tree-lined street with rows of brownstones on both sides. The sun had already set, but the streetlamps cast a soft light over the surroundings.

Margaret sat quietly in the passenger seat. She looked at the door handle, then back to David's dark features. His face was ruggedly handsome, and he was starting to grow a beard. When he gazed at her face with his golden hazel eyes—like the color of a cat's—she could see that he felt contrite.

"Listen, David, I'll stay out of Kevin's way more often. Give him more room to work, if you'll cover his back," she said in a half plea.

"Yeah," David smiled. "That's what I do, Margaret. Remember, I saved his ass before, I'll do it again if need be."

"Thanks," she said sounding relieved, as she pulled on the door handle to exit the car.

"I'll stay till I see that you're safely inside," David offered. He got out and stood by the driver's side, looking over the top of the vehicle as Margaret closed the door.

"Thank you," she said before she turned and trotted up the stairs to the front door of her brownstone. After fumbling with the keys, she opened the door partway, turned back to give David a quick wave and then slipped inside.

Suddenly, a pair of strong hands grabbed David roughly by the shoulders and spun him around. David found himself face to face with Blanchard, who had snuck up behind him—accompanied by one of his lackeys, who was on standby mode. Blanchard stepped forward, driving a stiff jab to David's solar plexus that sent him collapsing to his knees.

"You break into my house!" Blanchard growled after glancing up and down the block to make sure nobody was watching. "You take my gun? Did you find Osterman's—or any other bodies—connected to my gun?!"

David could do nothing on his hands and knees in the middle of the street but pant like a dog, struggling to maintain consciousness.

"If you want war, you've got it, Allerton."

"We—we know," David gasped, "you… killed… Osterman."

"What are you talking about?" Blanchard, red-faced with fury, knelt down on one knee so he was right in David's face. "I didn't kill him, and I don't know who's trying to convince you that I did."

"The… evidence," David, still winded, managed to say.

"What evidence? All you've got on me is that I was running a protection racket. It was me looking the other way and letting them deal in our area. That was it. I wasn't muscling them or anything. We were businessmen, conducting business. Then Osterman comes to me and he says, 'Sly, I can't come up with the money this quarter.' "

"And—and you killed him." David was slowly getting his wind back.

"I didn't even threaten him. Ask his partner—he was there—and so was Two Smooth. I gave him credit for the quarter."

David looked directly into Blanchard's piercing gray eyes in the light from the streetlamps. With his fierce expression and meticulous crew cut, he looked like a hard-core Marine. He was a man who easily peeled off sixty pushups every morning and ran a mile every day—and his punch proved it.

His eyes proved something else to David.

"I believe you," David said as he shook his head, trying to pull himself together. "But if you didn't, who did?"

"Hmmm—" Blanchard seemed to ponder the question as he got to his feet, towering over David. "If I were you, Detective, I would think back on who put the idea in your head to chase me. I suggest you look deeper into that dead girl's life."

"You think she has something to do with Osterman's murder?"

"Well, I can tell you something that you obviously don't know—it certainly wasn't because of the dope. The dope is what kept us glued together. There was plenty to go around. Those Wall Street types have scads of money and big noses."

Blanchard gestured to the cop waiting nearby, who came closer on cue. He was a dark-complected Middle Eastern with long, straight hair. David assumed he was Shah Isharri.

"Why would someone want us to think it was you?" David asked as he rose unsteadily to his feet. Still weak-kneed, he leaned against the side of his car for support.

"Stupid question," Blanchard said. "Look, Allerton, you're barking up the wrong tree here, and you're wasting time while the real killers are getting away. Interview the dead girl again. You'll find your answers there, I'm sure."

Having completed their mission, Blanchard and Isharri turned around and walked over to a car parked on the other side of the street.

"Interview a dead girl?" David grumbled under his breath as he got into his car.

SIGHT TO THE BLIND

David sat across from Mary at an Indian restaurant on the Lower East Side. She was busy tearing away pieces of flatbread and dipping it into one of the three sauces on the table. David didn't know if it was her metabolism, or the coke, but she was a voracious eater. Her long brunette hair was curly with a perm which enhanced the sculpted quality of her strong chin and jawline.

David let his eyes wander down the straps of Mary's dress—from her creamy shoulders to her alluring cleavage. He liked the erection she stirred in his slacks.

She stopped eating abruptly and looked up at him with her dark eyes. "Why so quiet?"

David mulled over his thoughts for a moment. "I have some very important questions to ask you. I want you to answer them as truthfully as you can."

Mary, reaching for another piece of flatbread, quickly retracted her hand when she heard the uncharacteristically serious tone in his voice. "What do you want to ask me?"

"Truthfully, now."

"Yes—go ahead."

"What do you know about Pamela Walker?"

Clearly annoyed, she rolled her eyes and frowned at David. "She was a snow bunny."

"Is that all? I don't want you to leave anything out," he persisted.

"Well, I always saw her with the rich guy, always holding onto him. She did whatever he asked her to do—like a trained puppy."

"By the rich guy, you mean Osterman?"

"Yeah, him," she said flatly.

"She did *whatever* he said?"

"Whatever he said—yes."

"Isn't there anything else?"

Mary pursed her lips as she pondered the question in silence.

David stole a frustrated glance at her and sighed. He felt like he was dealing with a 'blonde' moment.

"She and the Witch had a big fight one night," Mary finally said.

"The Witch?"

"Osterman's ex."

"Ms. Hendricks?"

Mary replied somewhat impatiently, "Whatever her name is."

"Well, go on," he prodded.

"Something to do with money, or jewelry. Something that brought the fight to a party one night. Came down to a catfight. The two of them had to be separated."

"How long ago was this?" David asked her eagerly.

"A long time ago," Mary rolled her eyes again, and then reached for the bread. "About a year ago, I guess."

"What else?"

"What else, *what?*" she said, sounding exasperated.

David decided to just sit back and watch her eat for a while. When the waiter came with their plates, Mary leaned back to put a napkin on her lap. David was still ruminating on her statements. She had to have seen something. How else was he to interview a corpse?

"There is someone who would know much, much more about Pam," Mary said as she picked up a fork and attacked her entree.

"Who's that?"

"Karen Francis, of course." Then she pointed at his plate with her fork. "Aren't you going to eat?"

Kevin pulled his car to a stop in front of the Brooklyn apartment house where Karen Francis lived. It was almost dusk, with the last rays of sun fading from the city street. Kids were still out playing, and they charged past Kevin as he approached the building and climbed the narrow steps to the front door. In the vestibule, he pressed the button next to her name several times, but there was no response. Finally, Kevin decided to ring the superintendent to get in.

The super was a stocky middle-aged man with chiseled features and a gray goatee who asked Kevin what he wanted.

"I need access to apartment 3B," Kevin said, pointing over the superintendent's shoulder.

"And, who are *you*?" the superintendent asked, frowning a little at being disturbed.

Kevin could see in the superintendent's hands that he had been working on a doorknob assembly with a screwdriver. With his sleeve, he wiped at the sweat on his brow.

"My name is Kevin Whitehouse. I'm here on an urgent police—" Kevin broke off as he reached into his jacket for his ID, "—matter. I need to speak with Karen Francis, but she doesn't answer her buzzer. She may be a victim of foul play."

"Cops! Again with you guys. When do you quit?" Without waiting for an answer, the super turned and marched away from the vestibule door, snatching a large ring of keys from a hook on his belt at his side.

"When the case is solved," Kevin replied with surprising calm.

The superintendent strode up the stairs with heavy footfalls. Kevin followed right behind him. When he reached the door to 3B, the super searched through the keys until he found the one he wanted. "You guys never, ever stop. What did this girl do now?"

"Cops have been here before?" Kevin asked, surprised.

"A lot, mister. The woman is a prostitute," he replied disdainfully. "Didn't you know that?"

Kevin nodded, as various thoughts went through his head: like the super was a nosy cuss. Since it was unlikely that anyone in the investigation had approached him, the guy was probably eavesdropping.

The superintendent unlocked the door and opened it wide.

Once inside, Kevin and the superintendent froze—the living room had been ransacked. The couch pillows were flung about, a corner table was knocked over, the contents of a bookshelf were on the floor, and a throw rug was bunched up against the wall.

"Go downstairs," Kevin told the super, "and call the police. Tell them to get here ASAP—that it's an emergency."

The super nodded, backed away several steps, then turned and went briskly down the stairs.

Kevin stepped cautiously into the hallway that led to the other rooms. He could see that the pots and pans in the kitchen were strewn about, and a small television was on the floor, knocked down from a stand near the table. The cupboards were left open, their contents pulled out onto the floor.

As he turned back to the hallway, he called out Karen's name, but there was no answer. He peered into the bathroom. The tub was empty, thank God. Other than the upended hamper—the clothes now in a heap on the floor—the room appeared relatively undisturbed.

"Karen?" he called again. Kevin stopped to listen for any sound at all in the apartment, but there was none.

Reluctantly, he approached the bedroom—the closed door filled him with dread. As Kevin reached for the doorknob, he wished he had David behind him, carrying a gun. In fact, if he had known what would be waiting for him here, he would have sent David instead.

Finally, Kevin turned the knob, pushed the door open and saw what he most feared to find. Karen lay across the bed on her back, staring up at the ceiling blankly, her mouth agape. The bedroom was torn apart like the rest of the apartment: the dresser drawers had been pulled out onto the floor, and the closet doors were open—her clothes strewn everywhere. Clearly, someone was searching for something.

The sheets on the bed were crumpled up around Karen's head. The right side of her face, near the cheekbone, was marred by a large bruise. Her body was splayed out, clad only in a short nightshirt. Kevin approached the bed slowly. He noticed there were more bruises on the pale skin around her neck as he touched her there to check for a pulse. There was none.

Kevin left the room abruptly—stepping carefully over debris—and exited the apartment. Once he was outside the door, he could hear the police radios squawking as they entered the vestibule of the apartment building to speak with the super, who was waiting for them.

A few moments later, Kevin could hear the cops start up the stairs. He leaned over the wooden railing, and looked down absently as he waited for them to materialize, preoccupied with the thought that their one opportunity to interview the corpse of Pamela Walker was now a corpse herself.

Kevin spoke with the cops who, after taking a cursory look at the crime scene, called in two detectives and the forensics squad. Since the precinct was located nearby, they all arrived together in what felt to Kevin like no time. After exchanging some basic information with the detectives to explain his reasons for being there—and giving them his card in case they had any further questions—Kevin hurried down to his car and drove off. He headed for the Brooklyn Bridge and then downtown Manhattan. There was only one other way that Kevin knew of to interview a corpse.

***

The officer led Kevin into the evidence room. It was empty except for the single table and chair. The fluorescent lights overhead cast a cold white light that hurt his eyes. Kevin took a seat at the table and waited until a clerk struggled through the doorway carrying a large, heavy box. He hauled it onto the tabletop and left without a word.

On top of the box was a chain of evidence slip. Kevin signed it and put it off to the side before he lifted the lid off the box. Inside were Pamela Walker's personal effects.

Kevin found a wide variety of objects: brushes containing strands of her hair, a few paperback books, a makeup kit, a stack of letters in envelopes addressed to RHB—which he set aside on the table—and two pairs of shoes. He also pulled out a clear evidence bag containing a few articles of clothing. The next item of interest he found was a diary that had probably once been locked, but now the clasp was broken. He opened it and scanned the first page. To his surprise, the large, loopy penmanship read "the diary of Karen Francis"—not "Pamela Walker."

Kevin rose, picked up the letters and the diary, and left the evidence room. He approached the same officer who had led him to the room earlier, and showed him the items he was holding. "Do you have copies of these?"

"Yeah, they've been copied and submitted to the file room," the officer answered.

Kevin smiled and returned to the evidence room.

Kevin, exhausted from the day's events, looked forward to being home. When he entered the apartment carrying two thick binders, he encountered a shocking sight. David and Margaret were in the living room watching television together. David was stretched out comfortably on the couch, legs crossed, hands behind his head, while Margaret reclined in a nearby chair.

"Hi, honey," she said, waving.

"Hey, Kevin," David said, not moving a muscle.

Kevin blinked. This scene, combined with everything else that had happened, was enough to make him keel over.

"Karen's dead," he stated flatly.

At this piece of news, David sat bolt upright. "What?!"

"When I went to interview Karen, I found her dead from manual strangulation. The preliminary forensic reports have borne that out as the cause of death."

"Do you know why she was killed?" David asked.

"No clue."

"That's terrible," Margaret said, getting up and going immediately to Kevin's side. "You poor thing—the discovery must been horrible for you."

Kevin headed toward the couch and sat down next to David, who had swung his legs around to make room for his buddy.

"What do you have there?" David asked, nodding at the binders.

"Some of Pamela's personal effects. It seems that she had a secret admirer—she had stacks of letters from him. And oddly enough, she had *Karen's* diary in her possession. I found it in the evidence box. These binders contain the copies."

David took one of the binders from Kevin and started flipping through the pages.

"Diary?" Margaret walked over and took the other binder from Kevin's lap. "Let me see it."

Kevin rested his head against the back of the couch. "Have at it, guys."

"RHB?" David queried, pointing at the binder. "These letters are all addressed to RHB. So are the copies of the envelopes. Do you know of anyone involved in the case who has those initials—or any-thing close to them?

"Beats me. It's obviously not Pamela Walker," Kevin said.

"How do you know that?" Margaret asked, paging through the diary.

Kevin sighed, feeling tired and exasperated. "Margaret, it's RHB—not PW."

"Maybe it's her nickname."

"She's got a point there," David said.

Suddenly, Kevin sat up straight on the couch and looked first at David and then Margaret.

"What game are you two playing now?" he asked suspiciously.

"What are you talking about, Kevin?" Margaret asked.

"You two agreeing with each other and not fighting—" Kevin pointed to the television, which was still on, albeit at low volume, "—and watching TV together? What's going on here?"

David, his eyes still on the binder pages, replied, "We called a truce for now. Until the end of the case."

"The end of the case, huh?"

"Yeah," Margaret said. "This is a tough one. We need to put our heads together, not bang them against each other."

"I see." Kevin, apparently mollified, relaxed his position on the couch. "Well, what's our next step?"

"It's time to apply muscle," David said. "I'm going to find out who this RHB is. I figure once we know that, we might get a better handle on the case."

"I think we also have to find out why the killer tossed the apart-ment," Kevin added.

"Maybe they were looking for these letters," David said as he turned another page.

"Possibly," Kevin felt his eyes droop with exhaustion. "I think I'll go take a nap." He rose to his feet with effort and stepped over to Margaret, who he kissed on the cheek before heading to his bedroom.

"Goodnight, sweetheart," Margaret called after him.

"I'm outta here." David rose and grabbed a jacket out of the closet. He stashed the binder under his arm when he reached the door.

Margaret looked bewildered. "Where are *you* off to?"

"Gonna bash in a few skulls," David replied, and slipped out of the apartment.

Margaret refocused her attention on the diary, this time starting at the end.

Claire Montague was on her way to the front door to her home in St. Albans, Queens, when she noticed a large shadow on the doorstep had preceded her. She slowed her pace to a stop and frowned in the darkness as she called, "Hello?" When no answer was forthcoming, she held up her keys and pressed a button on the fob that turned on the exterior lights, so that the doorstep was brightly illuminated. There she saw David leaning on one of the pillars that held up the porch roof.

"Oh, it's you, Mr. Allerton." Claire sighed with relief. She walked past him to unlock the front door. "What can I do for you tonight?"

"I need to ask you a stupid question."

"Sure, come on in." As she entered her house, she held the door open for David to follow.

David closed the front door behind him and followed her into a comfortably furnished living room. Gesturing to the binder he held in his hand, he got right to the point: "I'm trying to find out who RHB is."

After carelessly tossing her handbag on the couch and stripping off her jacket, Claire turned around to face him. "Who?"

"RHB. I have a whole bunch of letters that were written to an

RHB, but I don't know who she is. See—" David opened the binder and handed it to Claire.

She took it and looked down at the pages, and in an instant her face brightened.

"I don't know who RHB is, but I *can* tell you this: that's Stewart MacDonald's handwriting."

Really!" David exclaimed. "There was no return address on any of the copies of the envelopes."

"Well, this is definitely Stewart's handwriting—that scrawl on the bottom is his signature."

"Damn!" David said, obviously startled by a sudden realization. "Damn!" he repeated.

"What?"

"What if Stewart MacDonald had a love affair with Pamela Walker, too."

"I seriously doubt that." Claire turned another page in the binder. "Whoa, this is some pretty hot stuff. Stewart must have been pretty smitten."

"Why do you doubt it, then?" Claire shrugged, but couldn't seem to take her eyes off the letters. "Because Hugh and Pam were like Frick and Frack. They were *very* close. So close that I couldn't get between them, and believe me, I tried. Anyway, I can't see Stewart doing anything like that—how could he cheat around his business partner? Wouldn't he worry that Hugh would find out?"

"People do strange things when it comes to drugs and sex, Ms. Montague."

"And obviously, this RHB is not Pamela. Those aren't her initials."

"Maybe it's her nickname?" suggested David, hopefully.

Claire nodded. "There actually was a lot of that going around. Even I have one."

"What is it?"

"Sweet Sexy Thing."

"Hmm," David said, pondering the idea as he looked her over. "I see."

Finally, Claire closed the binder and handed it back to David. "That's definitely Stewart's handwriting, but unfortunately I can't help you with the identity of the recipient."

As David slipped the binder under his arm, he asked, "Do you know Pamela's nickname?"

Claire was quiet for a few minutes, deep in thought. "That's a good question."

"It's alright if you don't know. I mean, since we found the letters among her personal effects, it's a pretty safe bet that they might be hers."

"If you say so," Claire said noncommittally.

David nodded. "Well, thanks for the help, Ms. Montague."

"Hey, Mr. Allerton, would you like to stay for a drink?"

Surprised at the offer—and somewhat tempted—David resisted the impulse. "Maybe some other time, Ms. Montague. I've got to stay on top of the case."

"I understand. Maybe another time... Goodnight, Detective."

"Bye for now—and thanks."

David headed for the front door with her trailing. "What happens after this case is solved, Mr. Allerton? What happens to the good times?"

"Life goes on, I suppose." David opened the front door, glancing at Claire. "Good night, Ms. Montague."

"Goodnight, Detective."

Kevin was walking around in the apartment alone, clad only in his boxers, when his cell phone rang.

"Yeah, go ahead, David," Kevin said, after picking up the phone.

"I've got something to tell you."

"Where are you?"

"Heading over to Two Smooth's place. He might have some information we need."

"Okay."

"Hey, get this—the handwriting on the letters belongs to Stewart MacDonald."

"Get the fuck out of here," Kevin said, nonplussed.

"I'm telling you—it is."

"How do you know this?"

"Reputable source," David said, deliberately evasive.

"Margaret told me you were going out to bust some heads. Is that information from one of those?"

"No, no head-busting—yet."

"So why the call?" Kevin asked.

"I want you to go and brace this MacDonald character—confirm that he was the one writing the letters to Pamela Walker."

"Why would Stewart MacDonald write love letters to Ms. Walker? Wasn't that his partner's squeeze?" Kevin sounded puzzled.

"It's *his* handwriting. See if he fesses up to anything," persisted David.

"Alright. Let me get some clothes on," Kevin said before hanging up.

The rap music was blaring as David was escorted to their destination by one of Two Smooth's thugs. He still had the binder with him. Unlike his last visit, when they conversed on the patio, he was shown into a den-like room, with a dartboard adorning one wall, a pool table in the middle and a bar to his left. The barstools had been moved to face the pool table. Perched atop them were three women dressed provocatively in tight, cut-off denim shorts, and semi-transparent silk shirts designed to reveal they were braless. One of them held a pool cue.

Two Smooth was strolling around the pool table, sizing up a shot while he chalked his pool stick. "Hello, Detective," he said, not taking his eyes off the table.

"Two Smooth," David replied as he entered.

"Make yourself a drink."

"Thanks." As David headed over to the bar, a striking brunette left her seat at the pool table in order serve him.

"What would you like?" she asked, leaning over the top of the bar and showing off her beautiful deep cleavage.

"Gin and tonic?" David asked.

The brunette turned and went to work on his drink.

"So, why are you back in my crib, my dude?" Two Smooth fired away with his pool stick, sending the number three ball into a side pocket.

"I've still got questions, Two."

"Always with the questions." Two Smooth still did not look up at David. Once again, he walked around the pool table, this time going behind a redhead seated on one of the stools. He smacked her on the ass with his pool stick as he passed by, causing her to jump down from the stool with a yelp.

"I'm in a jam, Two." David said, as the brunette set David's drink down in front of him on the bar. He thanked her and took a sip.

"What's the deal now?"

"I need to know nicknames."

"Nicknames?" Two Smooth finally looked up at David.

"*Nicknames*? Are you sure you're a detective or you just like hanging around with the Smooth?"

David grinned uncomfortably. "I have initials that I need a name for. I can ask you another way. What was Pamela Walker's nickname?"

"Walker—that was Hugh's girl, right?"

"Yeah, she was murdered the same time he was."

Two Smooth nodded, then returned to his pool game. "Candy Girl."

"Candy Girl?"

"Do I stutter, Detective?"

"CG."

"What's that?" Two Smooth sighted down the length of his pool cue, lining up his shot.

"Her nickname initials."

"Yeah, that sounds about right." Two Smooth took his next shot. The nine ball dropped into the corner pocket.

"Do you know whose initials are RHB?"

Two Smooth stood up straight from his shooting position and leaned back against the side of the pool table, pursing his lips, concentrating. "Shit, that's a good one."

"MacDonald has been writing love letters to this RHB. I'm trying to find her. I thought at first it was Pamela Walker, but it wasn't."

The redhead, back on the stool now, spoke up. "Sounds like it could stand for Red Headed Baby."

"What?" David and Two Smooth said in unison, and turned toward her.

"Yeah... it sounds like it's for the Red Headed Baby," she said, shifting uncomfortably in her seat.

"So," Two Smooth said. "Don't keep us in suspense, who is she? You?"

"No, baby, I'm your Carrot Top."

"Carrot Top—so who *is* the Red Headed Baby?" David prodded.

"Hmmm—" Carrot Top thought about it some more. "Karen—"

"Karen Francis?" David filled in, trying to suppress his excitement.

"Yeah, that's her." Carrot Top glowed from ear to ear. "Karen Francis. She's redheaded, too."

Two Smooth turned around to look at David, who came up alongside him. He opened the binder and rested it on the wood-grained edge of the pool table. He flipped through some pages and then stopped at one with an especially clear example of the signature. David pointed at it. "Is this MacDonald's signature?"

Two Smooth looked down and nodded. "That's his scribble."

"Fuck." David closed the binder and slipped it under his arm.

"Did you find out what you wanted?" Two Smooth asked.

"MacDonald had a relationship with Karen Francis. He was in love with a snow bunny."

"My snow bunnies are hot, my dude." Two Smooth leaned over the pool table, lined up a shot and fired the number one ball into the side pocket.

"This one is dead."

Two Smooth froze. "Wha—?"

"She was found dead earlier today. Strangled in her home, her crib tossed."

"Damn." Two Smooth straightened up. "I've got to hook up her mother with a funeral for her. That's the least I can do."

"You're such a gentleman, Two," David remarked, facetiously.

"Like I said, it is *the least* I can do."

David returned to the bar and swallowed big gulps of his drink.

"Are you thinking that Stewart popped Hugh and Pamela?" Two Smooth asked.

"I dunno. I don't have a motive. But then again, now I just might. But what could it be?" David shook his head, then downed another slug of his drink. "I'm not lying to you if I told you that I'm totally confused now. Both women were fucking your partners and now both of them are dead. Someone is covering their tracks."

"So you're no closer to the killer than you were when you first saw me." Two Smooth shook his head sadly.

"Maybe. Depends on what my partner comes back with."

When David came home, he found Margaret sitting on the couch, legs crossed, binder in her lap.

"Where's Kevin?"

"He's not here. He went to see MacDonald."

David strolled into the center of the living room. "Shit, I got news."

As soon as the words were out of his mouth, Kevin came in the door. "What news?" he said eagerly.

David relayed the news about MacDonald and Karen Francis. Kevin was stunned, but Margaret was not impressed.

"That's not all," Margaret said. "This diary has some eye-popping information, too."

Both men turned toward Margaret.

"Well, don't keep us in suspense," David said.

"The diary clearly indicates that she was in a relationship with Stewart MacDonald, so we could have figured out the source of the letters from here—"

"Wait a minute," David said. "What the fuck is Karen's stuff doing with Pamela's stuff?"

"Karen probably threw the diary into the box with Pamela's personal effects when the police were collecting her stuff," Kevin said. "She needed to hide it because the killer was looking for it."

"That's why her home was tossed!" David exclaimed, pointing at

Kevin.

Margaret pressed on with her findings. "Karen mentions a rivalry between Deborah Hendricks and Pamela Walker, says the two got into a big catfight in the club right in front of everyone. It took three bouncers to pry them apart."

"Pamela had a hard time with Ms. Hendricks, hmmmmm," Kevin headed over to his laptop and sat down in front of it. "What are we looking for here?"

David turned to Margaret. "They had a fight—so what?"

"I haven't finished it yet, but this diary mentions *several* confrontations. These women clearly didn't like each other."

"Does it say why?"

"Pamela did everything she could to demean Deborah Hendricks in her husband's eyes. That's how she got him to divorce her. She literally replaced his wife one zing at a time."

Running his hand over his razor stubble, David mumbled almost to himself, "Hmm… bad blood between these two women—"

"More shit, though," Margaret continued. "Then Karen catches Stewart MacDonald's eye, and he falls for her and starts in with the love letters."

"So, MacDonald was banging a snow bunny, big deal," Kevin said.

"But that was when Karen found out that Stewart MacDonald was also banging Deborah Hendricks. Apparently, he successfully kept both affairs under the radar."

"Damn," David said. "Two women not knowing that they are fucking the same man?"

"But Karen found out. MacDonald must have screwed up somewhere," Margaret added.

David paced back and forth. "So he gets greedy. MacDonald offs his partner to get control over the entire network—"

Kevin piped up, "But why kill Pamela?"

"Pillow talk," David answered.

"What?!" Kevin and Margaret chimed in together.

"When do you jabber-jaw the most?"

Kevin had an epiphany just then: "Hendricks and MacDonald each planned to kill off their rivals."

"And what about Karen Francis?" Margaret asked.

"MacDonald now runs the show, he runs everything. MacDonald is the Man. He's too far above little Karen—he's not going to give her any more, and maybe he gave her less. She was just a squeeze. He really wants Hendricks—to him, she's the prize."

"So Karen threatens to tell her?" Margaret closed the binder and tossed it on the couch next to her.

"It's the only thing that makes sense—the most logical explanation," Kevin said. "She threatens to reveal their relationship to Hendricks. She has all of his handwritten letters as proof."

"She senses danger—expects her home to be ransacked," David said, picking up their theoretical trajectory. "So when the police asked her for Pamela's stuff, she hid her diary and the letters along with it. What better place to hide them than in the evidence room of a police precinct?"

"When MacDonald visits one day, he starts tossing her home because she refuses to give him the letters. He threatens her and then strangles her, but he finds nothing in the apartment," Margaret concludes. "But wait—do you think MacDonald did it himself or was it a cop?"

Kevin said, "I vote for the cop theory."

"I don't know—" came from Margaret.

"I think it was MacDonald himself," David said. "And I no longer believe that a cop killed Osterman, either."

"Based on what?" Kevin asked.

"A gut feeling."

"I still think MacDonald was the mastermind but not the killer," Kevin persisted.

"Why don't you go and brace him then, see if he spills the beans."

"I'd rather gather the evidence and go to Jefferies."

"He'll tell you to come back with *real* evidence," David countered.

"We have the phone records between Hendricks and MacDonald on the day of the murder," Margaret interrupted.

"That's not going to work. They talked like that almost every day." Kevin sighed.

"Jefferies is just going to turn you around at the door," David ventured. "You're walking into a nosebleed. I'm going to review our evidence to see if we can tighten up our theory."

"I'll help," Margaret added, as she rose to follow him into the kitchen.

"You'll do *what?*" Kevin asked, astonished.

Margaret stopped in front of the kitchen doorway. "Help."

"Help *David?*"

"Yes. Four eyes are better than two."

"What's going on between you two, anyway?"

"I told you already—a truce. So, are you going to join us for the fun?"

"Hell, no. I'm going to Jefferies," Kevin explained as he stood up to leave.

"Before you go, I got one for you," Margaret said. "Why would Blanchard kill Karen Francis?"

"He killed her for MacDonald," he said evenly. "MacDonald hired him to do it—he's too weak to kill or shoot anyone."

"But why would Blanchard become a contract killer?"

"For the money, babe—for the money."

"Oh, well then—go with your theory. We'll test them both."

"I'll be back in an hour. Try not to stab each other before I get back." Kevin smiled at her as he left the apartment.

"Where is the gun? Where are the fingerprints in the house? Where is the evidence, Kevin?" Jefferies asked, sitting back in his chair.

"I know it's mostly circumstantial—"

"Mostly? You've got to be kidding me, Kevin. You were once a cop—you know the DA won't proceed on the basis of anything as flimsy as this. He'll bounce the investigation right back at us."

"It's too thin?"

Jefferies sat up and looked squarely at Kevin. "Have you been to see Dr. Fagen? I think you need to see him today."

Kevin, shaking his head, said, "No, I don't need to see Fagen."

"I think that you do," Jefferies insisted.

Kevin headed over to the couch and plopped down into it, sighing tiredly. "What makes you think that I need to see the doctor?"

"Kevin, you are on a complicated case. I need you running on all four cylinders. I think you're running on two."

"Right."

"Just drop in on Fagen. That's all I'm asking. Just go in and say hi to the guy."

"Just to humor you, I'll do it," Kevin said as he hauled himself off the couch and headed to the door. "I'll be back with more evidence, Sam."

"You do that," Jefferies said as Kevin closed the door behind him.

About two beats later, Jefferies picked up the phone, punched in a number and waited. "Dr. Fagen? Yeah, this is Sam Jefferies. I think Kevin Whitehouse is coming your way." He listened to the reply and added, "I need you to help him—I can't have a crazy man cracking this case."

Kevin strolled into Dr. Fagen's office. "Hey, doc!"

Fagen was sitting behind his desk, looking through a patient's file. When Kevin approached him, he sat up and removed his glasses, resting them on his desk.

"Kevin, it's nice to see you again." Fagen stood up and extended a hand.

As Kevin closed the distance between them to shake it he said, "How have you been doing, doc?"

"Have a seat, Kevin." Fagen gestured to the chair in front of his desk. Kevin sat down in it.

"I'm doing fine, Kevin." Fagen retook his seat. "I should ask you the same question."

"I'm working on this tough case, and I'm a little mixed up about it now. You know the case: Osterman and Walker?"

"I've heard about it."

"Doc, have you talked with Sam Jefferies?"

"Why do you ask?"

"Every time—well, *almost* every time I go to see him, he pipes up about me seeing you."

"That's because we're all concerned about you," Fagen said, smiling fondly at Kevin.

"Maybe this concern is a little misplaced?" Kevin suggested.

"Have you been taking your medication like I've asked you to?"

"No, I stopped taking that stuff. I don't need it."

"Yes, you do need it, Kevin." Fagen sighed. "Do you know why you're supposed to take it?"

"It balances my brain chemistry—shit like that."

"It keeps you from seeing things."

"But that's just the problem, doc. I don't see anything."

"Do you remember why I'm your doctor, Kevin?"

"Because you believe—mistakenly—that there is something wrong with me."

"Kevin, you had a serious blow to the head. You were hospitalized as a result. Do you remember that?"

"Yeah, doc. Tell me something that I don't know," Kevin said flippantly.

"You have multiple personality disorder."

"What? What's that?"

"You've obviously forgotten about your sessions here, Kevin. I have to tell you so you'll understand. Listen to me, please."

"Yeah, doc?"

"David Allerton does not exist. He is a side of you that you invented because you could not handle the more violent aspects of police work. Since you could not do them, you created David Allerton to do them for you."

"Doc, you're confused. David Allerton is as real as you or me."

"Only to you, Kevin."

"You're wrong, doc. Others see him—he even has a girlfriend. Is she manufactured by my brain, too?"

"Kevin, *you* are David Allerton."

"How can that be, doc? David is black and from Brooklyn. Physically fit, ex-Marine, martial arts—all that stuff. I don't know anything about those things—*and* I'm not black and I'm not from Brooklyn."

"David's history has been manufactured by you. Everything about him is from you."

Kevin shook his head. "Doc, you're crazy."

Fagen, confident that he had Kevin's attention now, relaxed in his chair. "You needed David Allerton to do all the things you believe you can't."

"Who's fucking his girlfriend?"

"You are, Kevin."

"Who's fucking Margaret?"

"Who is Margaret?"

"My girlfriend."

"I can only assume you are."

Kevin sat back in his seat, his body seeming to deflate. "I have to go, Dr. Fagen."

"Kevin, please, start taking your medication. You must, or you will continue to see David."

"I've got a case to work on—with David."

"That's just the problem, Kevin—you working this case."

Kevin rose. "What are you talking about, doc?"

"You are mentally unstable, Kevin. If that information gets out and you're not taking your medication, it could negatively affect the outcome of the case. We need you stable—not as a tool for the defense so they can have the case thrown out."

"Crazy cop cracks case, huh?"

"That's just about it, Kevin."

Kevin rounded the chair and headed for the front door.

Fagen stood up. "Kevin!"

Kevin stopped and turned around. "Yes?"

"I have a challenge for you."

"What do I get out of it?"

Fagen ignored the question. Instead, he opened one of his desk drawers and produced a pill bottle. He opened it, shook out two pills in his hand and held them out to Kevin. "If you believe you're right, then you won't be afraid to take these pills and have lunch before you go home."

Kevin looked at Fagen. "I repeat—what's in it for me?"

"You never have to come back and see me again."

Kevin thought it over. "Pills, lunch, and then home."

"Yes. Take these pills, go and have lunch, and then go home."

Kevin ruminated on this a while, then went over and took the pills from Fagen's hand, popping them into his mouth. "I tell you, you're wrong, doc." Kevin extended his hand once again. They shook hands as Kevin said, "I'll be seeing you."

"Yes, Kevin. You will."

UPSETTING AT THE LEAST

When Kevin got home, he went straight to the kitchen and found nobody there. The table was still covered with photos and reports, as well as one neat stack of documents pushed over to one side. Kevin went through it, and discovered that David and Margaret had been busy. They had isolated just the reports and photos that would prove their hypothesis that Stewart MacDonald was the shooter.

Kevin knew better: to him, the killer had all the earmarks of a professional. The monkey wrench in his theory was the fact that the killer fucked Pamela Walker. But on some level, that was easy to understand. A hot little honey, face flushed from fear, begging not to die. Her rape would be a final humiliation before her death, a donkey punch with some kick. Her orgasm would be her finish.

Or maybe the fucking was some form of revenge. But if the killer was Blanchard, why would he do that? He had no personal connection to her—he probably would have just pumped bullets into her chest.

On the other hand, MacDonald was in revenge mode for the sake of his lover, Deborah Hendricks. She was probably giving him some quality pussy. But now, it was the money that did it for MacDonald. He was greedy. With Osterman out of the way, he would be in full control of the corporation. Well, no, not if Hendricks gets Osterman's estate when he dies. They had no children, so the assets go to both Hendricks and MacDonald—the royal couple.

But Blanchard gets no love—if he was involved, he was a dupe, just a paid mercenary. Could Margaret and David be right?

Kevin went to the bedroom, stripped down to his boxers, and called Margaret at her apartment, but there was no answer. So what? She was probably out. Kevin crawled into bed and fell asleep.

When he awoke the next morning, Kevin slid his feet onto the floor and yawned. He rose and found he had the urge to take a leak right away. While watching the stream of urine, his thoughts started drifting and then locked on his penis.

His urine.

"David!" he called out. No answer.

He finished pissing and headed to David's room, where he flung open the door, and found it empty. Fuck, probably with that snow bunny again!

Next stop, the kitchen table, where he impatiently rifled through the documents, searching for the forensics reports. He couldn't find it.

Then his attention was caught by that neat stack of paper he noticed the previous night—and started flipping through it. Inside he found Pamela Walker's forensics. Ten cc's of type B negative secretor's semen was found in her vagina.

Type B negative.

Kevin had found his shooter.

He retrieved his cell phone from the bedroom and called Jefferies. He would need two things: Blanchard's blood type and a court order to get MacDonald's.

Kevin arrived at One Police Plaza in the late afternoon. He encountered Jefferies in the lobby conversing with some people. Jefferies broke away from the group once he saw Kevin.

"That's a lot of shit you asked for this morning, Kevin. Are you onto something?"

"I don't know why I didn't think of it earlier. We have the blood type of the killer," Kevin said excitedly. "He was a secretor."

"Yeah, that's right—a pro would have used a condom, taking the evidence with him."

"Rookie killer then?" Kevin asked.

Jefferies shrugged. "Pros make errors too."

They were at the bank of elevators now, and Jefferies punched the up button. When the doors slid open, they stepped inside.

"So you think the killer is either Blanchard or MacDonald?"

Kevin nodded. "One of them whacked Osterman and Walker. My bet is that it's Blanchard. Once we determine who it is, we'll also know who killed Karen Francis."

"What if the semen was planted by a pro?" Jefferies raised an eyebrow. "Have you ever thought of that?"

"It would be dead semen." Kevin shook his head. "No, this was so fresh it still had motility. Read the forensics."

"I'm sure you did."

The elevator doors opened. They walked briskly to Jefferies' office. Once behind his desk, Jefferies sat down, picked up the phone and made a call. Kevin took the seat directly across from him.

"Yeah," he said, "I want to speak with Susan Ito." Looking at Kevin, he asked, "Have you spoken to her lately?"

"Who?"

"Susan."

"Susan Ito?"

"Yeah, who do you think I'm talking about?"

"No, why?"

Jefferies shook his head. "Yeah?" he said into the phone. "Susan, I need those blood types. Yeah. Do we have a match? Uh huh, uh huh, yeah. Thanks." He hung up the phone, and took a seat.

"C'mon, Sam, don't leave me hanging," Kevin pleaded.

"Barking up the wrong tree again, brother." Jefferies leaned back in his chair. "MacDonald is type A positive, Blanchard is O positive, and your killer is B negative."

Kevin's shoulders sagged.

"I didn't think it would be that easy," Jefferies said. "Well, now at least we know who's a waste of time. No need to bother Blanchard or MacDonald anymore."

Looking downcast, Kevin said, "That was my best and only lead. It proves that even David and Margaret were wrong."

"Margaret?"

"My new girlfriend."

Jefferies nodded.

"She's helping us," Kevin added.

"You mean to tell me you're giving her access to official information about an ongoing case?" Jefferies said, visibly upset.

"It's alright—she's good. Her role is just marginal, anyway. No problems there, I can assure you." Kevin waved dismissively at Jefferies.

"So what's your plan now? You said that was your last lead."

"Yeah—my last."

"What does David have?"

"Probably an assload of snow bunny right now. He didn't come home last night."

"He's sleeping with one of the suspects in this case?" Jefferies sounded perturbed again.

"She's not a suspect."

"You guys have got to learn to keep it in your pants."

"You know how David is, Sam. You can't tell—"

The phone rang. "Excuse me," Jefferies said as he raised the receiver to his ear. "Jefferies. Yeah. What? When was this? Really? Uh huh, uh huh. Have a blue and white ready for me downstairs with a good driver, Ferryman and Reynolds. I don't care, call them in. I want them here." Jefferies hung up the phone with a loud clatter.

"What's up, Sam?" Kevin asked, noticing the captain's exasperation.

"Westchester cops just called it in. Deborah Hendricks was found dead in her home."

"What?!"

"Found by her maid." Jefferies stood up to leave. "I'm going out there now. You coming?"

When Kevin followed Jefferies into Deborah Hendricks' home, he—like Jefferies—was stopped just outside the door and handed a pair of clear plastic booties to wear over his shoes before proceeding. The two, with Ferryman and Reynolds trailing behind, cut through the clusters of officers from New York and Westchester who'd already arrived. Members of the forensics team were all over the house, and police photographers were snapping pictures—the flashes temporarily blinding the onlookers.

The county sheriff led Jefferies into the living room, which was the epicenter of all the activity. The body of Deborah Hendricks was stretched out on the long couch, her robe thrown open, her dark hair over her face. Around her neck was a man's dark blue tie pulled taut—the flesh above the tie was pink, and below it was pale.

Jefferies, Reynolds, Ferryman, the sheriff and Kevin stood over her body—the technicians stepping away to give them room to stare down at her.

"Raped?" Jefferies asked the sheriff.

"We don't know yet," he said, and then added—as he gestured

toward the body—"But, look at her. I would guess that she was."

"I would guess you're right." Jefferies nodded in agreement.

"What do we have here?" Ferryman asked. "A serial rapist?"

"Someone who's not used to being around women with money," Kevin suggested. "Can you imagine fucking her in this living room?"

Everyone looked around at the high ceilings and chandeliers, plush leather sofas, gilt mirrors, and elaborately carved wooden chairs and tables.

"Probably watched himself and the victim in a reflection on the widescreen TV over there," Jefferies said, pointing to the huge black screen not far from the sofa.

"What if she had some lover come over and they had sex here on the couch? Reynolds said returning his gaze to the corpse.

"What?" Jefferies asked. "And she just laid there until the killer came and strangled here? Or maybe her lover strangled her."

"Mr. B negative strikes again," Ferryman said.

Finally, the five men backed away from the couch, allowing the technicians to resume their work on the area of the crime scene nearest the body.

"Shit, this makes five." Kevin sighed.

"You have an active killer out there," Ferryman said. He reached into his jacket and produced his pad and pen.

Jefferies looked at him dubiously, then said to Kevin, "Whitehouse, what do you think?"

"I don't know. I need more time to process this." Kevin looked discouraged.

"Are you tired of chasing blue uniforms?" This from Reynolds to Kevin.

"Are you tired of working on the force?" Jefferies quipped to Reynolds. "Come up with some leads of your own before you disparage others."

Reynolds took a step back, and looked away with a scowl.

"Well, this definitely changes things," Kevin remarked.

"Hold on—" Jefferies said to Kevin as he started to walk away; then turned around to add, "—follow me."

The two men went through a doorway in the living room leading to the den.

Kevin suddenly broke the silence. "I'm thinking MacDonald is the man with the pull now. Can you find out what happens to Osterman's estate now that his wife is dead?"

"Yeah, I can find that out," Jefferies produced his own pad and began to scribble.

Kevin reached into his jacket and showed Jefferies his IC recorder. "You really need to get yourself one of these, Sam."

"Whatever. So you think MacDonald is consolidating Osterman's assets?"

"Someone is." Kevin thought about it some more. "I think that either MacDonald is confident now that he can't be touched in the killing of his lover, *or* someone is bumping them off—all of them—and that MacDonald is next."

"Put MacDonald in protective custody?"

"No." Kevin shook his head. "I don't believe he's innocent. If this was just about drugs, then why kill Hendricks? If that were the case, the next logical victim would be Two Smooth."

"Right. He was the third wheel in their drug network," Jefferies agreed.

"No—I believe this is MacDonald's handiwork. He killed Deborah, his main squeeze, because she probably found out about his affair with Karen Francis." Kevin paused, and then added, "David and Margaret think that MacDonald is doing the killing himself, but now we know better. It's MacDonald who hired the triggerman."

"So how can we prove this?" Jefferies asked.

"I don't think we can. Unless we can find the triggerman and get him to roll over on him."

"Fat chance," Jefferies said.

"Why do you say that?"

"MacDonald is covering his tracks. How long do you think his triggerman is going to stay alive?"

"Not long, but that doesn't mean that I'm not going to find him."

Kevin climbed the stairs to his floor and stuck his key in the lock of his front door. The key was not lined up properly when he pushed in, striking against the lock cylinder instead. The door opened.

Kevin froze. "David?" he called. As he entered the apartment, he saw the back of someone sitting on his couch, watching the television.

"You need a better lock on your door, Allerton."

"Who are you?" Kevin asked, with some trepidation in his voice.

Blanchard got up from the couch and turned around to face him. "Get your gun. I've found your shooter."

"You what?" Kevin shook his head, pointing to Blanchard. "You're Blanchard, right? I've seen pictures of you filed in evidence."

"What?" Blanchard was taken aback. "I found your shooter, I said. You were right. He was a cop."

"Who, then?"

"Fucking Heidelman—the snitch," Blanchard said, almost spitting out his name. "I found out he was doing work for both Osterman and MacDonald."

"Work?"

"He was doing collection work for Osterman. Whenever a junkie wouldn't pay up, Heidelman would pay him a visit. He was getting twenty percent of all the funds he recouped for the network."

"How does that make him the triggerman?"

"He knew Osterman and his squeeze. He could have easily walked in and shot them both with no static."

"That would work."

"I looked over Karen Francis' forensics—" Blanchard reached into his jacket, coming away with two pieces of paper; he handed one to Kevin. "She was found with eight cc's of type B negative semen in her mouth."

"She gave the shooter head?"

"No, it was postmortem. Nothing was found in her esophagus or stomach."

"He strangled her and then came in her mouth?"

"His calling card."

"Fuck."

Blanchard handed over the second piece of paper. "Heidelman is type B negative."

With a gasp, Kevin said, "You found the shooter."

"Heidelman."

"Fucking rat."

"He was playing both sides against the middle when he thought you could make the racketeering charge stick. He doesn't need me—he did his own dealing behind my back."

"How did you find this out?"

"Another one of my detectives—his partner Shah Isharri—caught him, and Heidelman tried to lure him into the scheme. Isharri ran with him on some runs, but freaked when Heidelman bitch-slapped the wife of a debtor. These weren't dope heads, but Wall Street types that Heidelman was leaning on pretty violently.

"Isharri wanted to distance himself from the collection biz and came clean to me about it today. The fact that Heidelman went around me to cut a separate deal for himself was enough for me to suspect him of being the killer. No one kills like a cop—but you know that, don't you?"

"So what's your plan?" Kevin asked.

"Brace Heidelman, get him to roll on MacDonald and take them both in."

Kevin stood silently for a moment.

"C'mon, get your roscoe—we've got cop work to do," Blanchard said.

Kevin crossed the living room to the closet, opening it reluctantly. "Is there anyone else in the apartment?"

"Like who?"

"Like my roommate, David."

"What? You have another roommate named David? Nah, this joint is empty."

Kevin looked at Blanchard suspiciously. What was he doing? He was no field agent, capable of working with a seasoned cop like Blanchard. "Maybe we should wait for David."

Blanchard scowled. "Look we don't have time to wait for room-mates. What is he? A cop? A detective?"

Kevin looked uncomfortable as he filled him in. "He's a detective, like me."

"Get your roscoe and let's get this fucking guy, alright? Your friend can be on the next collar some other time."

Kevin reached up to the top shelf of the closet and produced a shoebox. Inside were two Glocks and four clips. He also took a leather shoulder rig from the closet and strapped it across his back. He then took a Glock and shoved it into its holster. He replaced the shoebox after taking an extra clip and shut the closet door.

"We're just going to go talk, right?" Kevin asked, swallowing hard.

"What are you? Afraid of your piece?" Blanchard scowled. "We're talking about bracing a killer cop. You'd better have your roscoe warmed up."

"I've got it."

"Well, come one—let's go to the Midnight."

Kevin was surprised when he saw his car parked on the street, since he assumed David had taken it to visit the snow bunny. He must have taken the subway instead. Kevin told Blanchard he'd drive them to the club. When he slid into the vehicle, Kevin noticed the binder with the photocopies of Stewart MacDonald's letters to Karen Francis on the passenger seat. David must have left it behind. Kevin tossed the binder into the backseat before unlocking the passenger door for Blanchard. He leaned forward to start the engine as Blanchard got in and made himself comfortable.

Blanchard turned to Kevin, "Did you fucking break into my house?"

Kevin shook his head. "It wasn't me—it was David's idea. He was the one who broke in."

"Who is this, David—your roomie? You said he's a detective?"

"Ex-cop." Kevin pulled the car out into the street and pressed down on the accelerator.

"Like you?"

"Yeah."

"Fucked-up pair." Blanchard looked out his window as the city slipped past.

"You can say that."

"I also have to say that getting my own gun in the mail spooked the shit out of me. Tell your partner that he sure knows how to freak out a cop."

"I'll be sure to do that."

***

The parking lot from the Midnight was packed with cars. Kevin drove past the lot and double-parked at the corner, on the darkened street across from the nightclub.

"We're going in?" Kevin killed the engine, punched on the hazards.

"Take the fight into the club? What are you, high?" Blanchard turned around, pointed to the parking lot down the street behind them. "I bet you that fuck parked in there."

He reached into his pocket and pulled out his cell phone, pressing a button and placing it against his ear. "Hey, you son of a bitch. Yeah. It's me. I need to talk to you, where are you?" Blanchard paused, then, "Where are you parked? That's what I thought. I'll meet you in the parking lot, then." Blanchard slapped his cell phone shut and pocketed it. "C'mon."

"You want me to come?" Kevin asked.

"What are you, shitting me?" Blanchard opened the car door and slid out into the night.

Kevin stepped out and joined the lieutenant, who was waiting for him on the sidewalk.

"You go around the back and hide in the shadows," Blanchard said, striking off down the block with Kevin at his side. "Keep an eye on the fucker. I'll brace him. If I have to pop him I will."

"You think that'll happen?"

"Do you think that he'll come quietly?" Blanchard gave Kevin a sidelong glance. "Come on, get with it. This guy is facing life in prison, and for a cop, that shit is a fate worse than the death penalty. If he thinks I'm here alone, he just might try something."

"So what do you want me to do?"

"Keep a motherfucking eye and ear open."

They entered the lot. Blanchard pointed further down, behind a row of parked cars. "Keep watch over there."

Kevin headed in that direction, and kept walking until he found a spot where he could hide in the shadows. He crouched down next to a car not too far off from where Blanchard stood, and peered through the driver's side window and windshield until he had an unobstructed view of him. He reached into his jacket and produced the Glock. It was remarkably light. He glanced at it for a moment, then turned his gaze back on Blanchard.

Heidelman emerged from across the street, passing under a streetlamp as he reached the sidewalk. He entered the lot and met up with Blanchard at the center. In the gloomy, streetlamp-lit night, Heidelman appeared taller than Blanchard, leaner, his suit fitting him loosely. Blanchard met him halfway of the main aisle down the middle of the lot. They spoke for a few moments.

Kevin ducked low, and moved in a very low crouch around the front of the car he hid behind and then down its length, until he was just two cars away from the two detectives. He peeked around the rear bumper of the car he leaned against, so he could see and hear the two detectives clearly.

"You were my boy," Blanchard said.

"I'm nobody's *boy*," Heidelman replied disdainfully.

"So you went to work for Osterman? And then you killed him?"

"You wearing a wire, Blanchard? You wouldn't wear a wire, would you?"

"Do you think I'm a squealer like you?" Blanchard replied hotly.

"It's hard to tell whose side you're on these days, boss." Heidelman glanced anxiously around the lot.

"Do you want to search me, or can we talk?"

Heidelman patted Blanchard for a wire, and found his gun instead.

"Don't think I'm giving you my piece," Blanchard said as he gripped Heidelman's fingers and squeezed them hard.

Heidelman retracted his hand forcefully and backed away. "What do you want to know, boss?"

"Did you kill Osterman?"

Kevin had retrieved his IC recorder from his jacket and turned it on, when he was suddenly grabbed from behind and pulled back from the bumper into the shadows between the cars. His feet scattered from under him, sending him to his rear. A hand covered his mouth, while the other grasped him by the wrist that held the Glock.

Kevin turned around with some difficulty to see David kneeling over him. David, placing a finger on his own lips as a sign for Kevin to remain silent, took the Glock from Kevin's hand.

"Where have you been?" Kevin hissed.

"I'm here looking for Mary," David whispered. "I saw the car, saw Blanchard, saw you." He motioned to the two men in the distance. "Blanchard helping you?"

"Yeah."

"What is he doing with Heidelman?"

"Heidelman's the shooter."

David's eyes widened. "No shit?"

"No shit," Kevin replied.

Both fell silent.

Heidelman seemed to relax, his legs spaced. He reached into a pocket and produced a pack of cigarettes. "Osterman was a fat cat fuck. He fucked up by turning in his own supplier. Greedy schmuck. Like the Colombians were going to deal with someone square that worked so underhandedly."

"Is that what MacDonald said?" Blanchard asked.

"Cigarette?" Heidelman handed the pack to Blanchard. Blanchard took it, slipped out a cigarette and gave it back. Heidelman took one for himself. "Yeah... Mac introduced me to the new math."

"The new math?"

"Yeah." Heidelman lit Blanchard's cigarette with a disposable lighter before he lit his own. "Erase Osterman, get a higher chair than you on the network."

"Osterman was your boy, though."

"My employer."

"Why rape the girl?"

"Who? Pam?"

"Yeah."

"MacDonald promised his bitch that she'd suffer before she died."

"His bitch?"

"Deborah Hendricks. She wanted the girl to suffer for fucking her husband."

"I see," Blanchard took a draw from the cigarette. "What about Karen Francis then?"

"She was fucking Mac and threatened to blackmail him for coke. Can you believe that? Fucking snow bunny would rather blackmail someone for flake than cash."

"Blackmail him how?"

"Mac was dumb enough to tell her that he was sleeping with Hendricks. Everyone knew what a jealous, crazy bitch Hendricks was, especially Karen Francis. What she didn't know was that Mac was going to get rid of her, too," Heidelman said smugly.

"Mac was cleaning out the women from his life."

"That was his plan. He felt they were too unstable."

"So you strangled Karen Francis and fucked her in the teeth," Blanchard said, trying to hide his disgust at the thought.

"It's what I do, boss," Heidelman smiled, evidently finding humor in his evil deeds.

"When do you plan to do Hendricks?"

"I did her this morning. I raped her also. She had a hot body. I choked her during her orgasm, too. I thought that shit would be ironic. Her getting what she dished out."

"Balancing the scales of justice, eh?"

"Now what, boss? You going to turn me in?" Heidelman asked, no longer sounding so nonchalant.

"How can I? With what evidence?"

"I thought you'd see it that way." Heidelman took a drag from his cigarette. "How about this, boss? The new math."

"How does that work?"

"You're making chump change with your stupid protection racket. We move to collections instead, and get a higher seat in the network."

"Rubbing shoulders with drug dealers. I don't think so," Blanchard said with a note of condescension in his voice.

"Oh... so you have fucking scruples now?"

"More than you, Heidi, more than you."

"So what's your plan, you sanctimonious shit?" Heidelman didn't even try to hide the contempt he was feeling.

"Oh, so the nice guy gloves come off now, huh?" Blanchard flicked his cigarette to the side.

"You can say that."

Heidelman flicked his cigarette into Blanchard's face, sending a spray of embers across his eyes. Both men stepped back from each other and drew down. Heidelman's gun was drawn first, pumping seven shots into Blanchard's chest, fireballs lighting the night. Blanchard's gun discharged into the tarmac at their feet.

David sprung out with a leap from his hiding place, his gun out and firing at Heidelman. One shot tore through Heidelman's left shoulder, knocking him back and leaving him staggering. Still, he somehow found the wherewithal to fire back. David sidestepped the bullets aimed at him and continued to empty his Glock into Heidelman's chest, finally knocking him off his feet. David raced up to Heidelman and kicked the gun from his hand so it spun off across the tarmac, well out of the killer's reach.

Kevin came up behind David and together they approached Blanchard. David tore open his shirt, checked his bulletproof vest, and found four slugs and no blood. Blanchard was bleeding though, from the nose and mouth, and he squirmed with pain.

"Easy," David said as he squeezed his arm gently.

There was the sound of sirens in the vicinity.

"Is he going to be alright?" Kevin whispered to David so Blanchard couldn't hear him.

"Dunno."

"What about that guy?" Kevin said, pointing to Heidelman.

"Fuck him."

David sat in the hospital corridor looking at the IC recorder in his hand. He was listening intently to the playback with a small headset plugged into his ears. With the volume turned all the way up, he could hear cars passing, the wind, other ambient noise, as well as the broken English of two men conversing in the background.

"Hear anything of interest?" Kevin was sitting across the narrow corridor from him, in another row of seats that lined the wall.

David shook his head, barely letting his attention wander from the contents of the tape.

"Where the fuck were you for damn near two days?" Kevin asked, sounding irritated.

"I told you already, I was with Mary. What's the big deal?" David glanced up this time, meeting Kevin's eyes.

"Have you heard from Margaret?"

"No, why would I? Haven't you?" David asked. Then switching subjects, "Hendricks is dead?"

"Yes, her body was found this afternoon," Kevin said. He rose and started pacing in front of David.

"Strangled and raped by Heidelman. This fucker is some shit. I'm surprised that Blanchard let him get the drop on him like that."

Kevin stopped pacing long enough to reply. "Well, we got our shooter, we got our confession."

"Yeah, and we have three witnesses. You, me, and Blanchard—if he pulls through this okay."

"He'll pull through," Kevin assured him.

The two stopped talking when they saw Jefferies approaching.

"Blanchard?" David asked Jefferies without standing up from his seat.

"He'll make it." Jefferies took a seat across from David. "His vest caught all the bullets. He broke one rib and chipped another, but no internal organs were damaged."

"What about Heidelman?" Kevin asked.

"He's in surgery for a ruptured spleen, but it looks good for him too."

David remarked, "Lucky him, the—"

Before David could finish, Jefferies interjected. "Now my question to you is: what were you and Blanchard up to? What was this—vigilante justice?"

"No," David said, shaking his head emphatically. "We were there to lean on Heidelman, get him to talk."

"Did he?"

"Yeah, he confessed. He's definitely our killer," Kevin said.

"And he thought that Blanchard was the only one in the know."

"Probably."

"And who's the man behind the curtain? MacDonald?"

David answered this time. "Yeah. He's the mastermind, the one in charge."

"We have any evidence of anything?"

"Heidelman's blood type matches the semen found on the victims," Kevin said. "He was looking to slip by, thinking nobody would have suspected a cop as a killer."

"What now?" Jefferies asked.

"That's up to you and the DA, Sam," David said. "Work a plea deal with Heidelman. Get him to give up MacDonald."

"Good job. Real good job." Jefferies rubbed his face with both hands. He looked tired and drawn.

"Sam, maybe you should call it a night," Kevin suggested.

Jefferies sat back in the chair, deflated now. "What—you don't feel it?"

"Fatigue? A little. But I know where to go to get that taken care of," David said with a sly grin.

"Me, too. I'll see you guys later." Kevin was already heading over to the bank of elevators at the end of the corridor, while he pulled out his cell phone to call Margaret.

David watched his buddy walk off, and then turned back to Jefferies. "You think I'll need to give my testimony? When's the deposition?"

"I don't think that will be necessary." Jefferies rocked his body forward, over his knees and stood. "We have hard enough evidence for a conviction—unless there's any unforeseen problems. Did you meet with Fagen like I asked you?"

"Who?" David replied, indignant at the question.

"You—oh, wait. Gunplay. It's you, David, right?"

"What's that supposed to mean? Of course, it's me." Now David rose to leave, too, but not before adding, "Sam, you *definitely* need sleep."

"Yes, you're right. I need a wink or two." Jefferies clapped David on the back and guided him with a fatherly arm toward the elevators. "What do you say we go and have a coffee together?"

"Yeah, sounds good. I need to stay awake for a few more hours."

GOOD NIGHT, IRENE

The Midnight was near capacity. Bodies in dark silhouette moved frenetically to the rocking beat of the music. Multi-colored disco lights flashed their long beams rhythmically around the large dance floor. A burly guard waded through the crowd with David following closely behind. The two stopped when they reached a large private booth perched on a raised platform. David alone climbed the three steps that led to a circular space occupied by a round table, where Two Smooth sat, dressed in a suit, opened collar, no tie. In the crook of his arm was Claire Montague. They were flanked on both sides by members of his entourage—friends, associates, and snow bunnies.

"Detective," Two Smooth said.

"Mr. Allerton," Claire chimed in, letting Two Smooth know she was acquainted with David.

"Two, Claire," David replied, "mind if I sit down?"

"No problem." Two Smooth looked pointedly at the others seated around them and said, "Beat it for now. Scram." Claire, however, wasn't included in the evacuation.

Once the three were alone, David sat down next to Two Smooth in the circular, leather booth. "You heard what happened to Stewart MacDonald?"

Two Smooth took a leisurely sip of his drink. "He got sent up for a long time. I knew you'd catch him."

"Yeah," David said. "You knew I'd catch him. You sound like you knew it was him."

Two Smooth chuckled. "Did I?"

"Four counts of conspiracy to commit murder. MacDonald will be gone for quite some time," David nodded. "Leaving only one person to run the network."

"I wonder who?" Two Smooth asked innocently.

"Two Smooth, why don't you tell me the truth? You knew much, much more than you let on."

"I didn't let on anything, Detective. Remember—I didn't talk to you."

"You didn't at that. You just gave up information."

"Something like that. Hey, you're good. I knew you'd catch the bad guys."

"So you don't consider yourself a bad guy?" David persisted.

"Why would I think that?"

"Largely because MacDonald was your partner, and partners usually stick together," David explained calmly, trying not to reveal any sign of impatience.

"And?"

"I believe that MacDonald confided in you. I think he told you he was planning to kill Osterman—and he had your blessings. Largely because you weren't going to let MacDonald get away with it. Thereby helping me."

"Why would I do that?"

"Because that would leave you in charge of the network. You would be the top dog—Charles in Charge."

"That sounds interesting—" Two Smooth said, noncommittally.

"I'll go even further, Two. MacDonald told you about the letters, so you went with Heidelman and tossed Karen Francis' apartment. He couldn't have done everything that fast by himself—*and* rape and kill the girl at the same time. He had help."

"Really?"

"Did Heidelman even know about the letters?"

Two Smooth just stared at David with a blank expression.

"That's alright. You're above judgment. But now you know *we* know all about your network and how to take it apart."

"I think that's all wishful thinking, Detective."

David leaned forward to gaze directly at Claire. "The snow bunnies in this mess were in deeper than just coke and sex. Is that you, too, Claire? Were you in on this too, helping me out for Two Smooth here so MacDonald would get caught—so that your man could inherit the kingdom?"

"I don't know what you're talking about, Mr. Allerton," she replied, guilelessly.

David nodded. "Two Smooth, you are the good player in this, I have to admit. But if our paths ever cross again, I'll either be asking you for help or coming after you."

"I understand, Detective." He grinned a toothy, gold-laden grin.

"You get the club too, I suppose," he said, extending his hand to shake Two Smooth's.

"Yep," he confirmed.

David stood up. "Yes, indeed, you are a *very* good player, Two."

"Why, thank you."

David got up quickly and headed out, having first to wade through the thick crowd of patrons.

There was a knock on the front door. Kevin went over to open it and found Dr. Fagen facing him, smiling broadly.

"Kevin, can I come in?" he asked, sweetly.

"Yeah, doc. Anytime." Kevin stepped aside to let him in.

Fagen strolled into the living room and looked around. "Where's David?"

"Out somewhere. He said he had some fine-tuning to do on the case."

"So you haven't seen him recently?"

"I was with him two nights ago. Together we cracked a very important case—I couldn't have done it without him."

"Oh, really." Fagen gestured to the couch. "Mind if I take a seat?"

"Go ahead, doc. Make yourself comfortable."

Fagen took a seat on the couch. "I wanted to know how the medication has affected you."

"No effect at all," Kevin said as he sat down on the chair in front of his desk.

"So, let me ask you, did you see David at all while you were under the medication?"

"No, he was with his snow bunny."

"Are you sure about that?"

"That's what the man told me. He's been over there with her a lot, lately."

Fagen nodded. "And your girlfriend?"

"Margaret? She's probably at home."

"No," Fagen shook his head. "I meant while you were taking the medication."

Kevin thought about the question for a moment. "No, I didn't see her either. She probably had things to do."

"Kevin, do you know Susan Ito in the Medical Examiner's Office?" Fagen asked as he leaned forward in Kevin's direction.

"Yes, of course, I know her. She did a lot of work on this case we just busted."

"Do you remember being engaged to her?"

Kevin thought about that for a moment, the wheels in his head turning frantically, then: "No."

Fagen nodded and sat back again. "This Margaret, what's her last name?"

Kevin thought for a short minute and frowned. He must know that—but for some reason he couldn't remember it.

He looked at Fagen with some embarrassment. "I know I know it, but I just can't call it to mind right now, for some reason."

"How about David's girlfriend, do you know *her* last name?"

"Yeah—Mary Olman."

"Kevin, I have to tell you something important, and I want you to listen good. Your personality is beginning to fracture. As far as I can tell, there are three of you now. Three completely separate personalities that work either for you, through you or by you. Sometimes you see them apart from you, other times they're you. I think David has himself a girlfriend in the real world. I think Margaret is just another personality that you have concocted, to replace Susan Ito."

"Do you see that bookshelf over there?" Kevin said, indicating the bookshelf against the wall to Fagen's left. "Those are David's books. I don't know the first thing about them or what's in them. He does.

"Furthermore, do you see that closed door behind me?" Kevin swung his arm around, pointing at David's room in the hallway. "That's David's room—it's neat and tidy, which mine isn't. He sleeps in that bed. I've never slept in that bed in my life. How is what you say possible?"

Fagen sighed. "Kevin, you are complete individuals, the three of you. You each have a history, hobbies, likes and dislikes—but they all stem from you. Last year you were the ascendant personality. I see that you are no longer. You and David and now Margaret, switch up. Margaret probably less so."

Kevin shook his head. "What you're saying is complete madness. Margaret is real and she's seen David in the flesh. I've seen Margaret— shit, I sleep with Margaret!"

"She is all in your mind, Kevin. Since you were in that car accident where your partner was killed, you created David to do the things you feel you can no longer do. He's more physical than you are and more willing to expose himself to physical danger—and to do what's necessary in the face of it."

Kevin stood up. "It's time for me to get ready, doc. Margaret and I are going out to dinner. She'll be here in a few minutes."

Fagen rose from the couch, nodding. "I understand. It was nice talking to you, Kevin. Please keep in mind what I just said to you, and come and see me if you get the chance."

"Sure doc, it's been a pleasure."

David rang the doorbell, and almost immediately Cheryl opened the door.

"Detective," she said with a broad grin as David walked past her into the apartment.

"Where's Mary?" he asked.

"Right here!" she shouted from the bedroom.

"Would you like something to drink?" Cheryl asked.

"No thank you, Cheryl."

Mary emerged from her bedroom, dressed in a white blouse and a short black skirt; she had one high-heeled shoe on her foot and held the other in her hand. She leaned against the living room doorway and lifted her leg to don the other shoe. "I'm coming, I'm coming."

"You said that a lot last night too," David said with a smile.

"Can you get your mind out of the gutter?" Mary said, walking right into his arms. "Well, at least until later."

David planted a kiss on her. "C'mon, let's get moving."

They said goodnight to Cheryl as they slipped out the door.

When the doorbell rang, Kevin rose from the couch distractedly—he was still somewhat shaken over his conversation with Dr. Fagen. He looked cautiously through the peephole. On the other side he saw Margaret's smiling face. He swung open the door and stepped aside, allowing her to sweep in regally, as she usually did. She peeled out of her coat, revealing a short black dress with spaghetti straps.

"What are you doing?" she asked. "Aren't you getting ready?"

Kevin shut the door slowly. "Yeah," he said absently, as he reached over to pull one of her spaghetti straps down off her shoulder. She slapped his hand. It stung.

"We don't have time for that now, Kevin! Get your coat. God! The minute I put on something nice, you want to undress me."

She *was* real, Kevin thought, as she walked to the couch, turned around, and plopped down into it.

"What's the matter?" she asked him.

"What is your last name, Margaret?" His voice was low and sounded far away.

"Alexander, silly. You know that."

And Kevin did know that. He knew it before she opened her mouth. *Alexander, Margaret Alexander.* Yes, that was right. Why couldn't he remember it before with Dr. Fagen?

"Where do you live?" Kevin asked.

"Brooklyn Heights. What is this all about, Kevin?" she said, beginning to sound exasperated.

Kevin nodded. Yes, that was right too, she lived on Montague Street in Brooklyn Heights, a quiet, tree-lined street. He had been there several times. "Montague Street," he muttered.

"That's right." She stood up to approach him, taking him gently by the shoulders and looking directly into his eyes. "Is something wrong? What's happening with you?"

He shook his head. "Nothing, Dr. Fagen—"

She broke in to ask, "Did you see him today?"

"Yes, he came over."

She nodded. "And he said something about me?"

"No," he lied. "He didn't mention you at all."

"So what's the problem?"

"Nothing," he said, smiling now. "Let me get my coat." He turned around and headed to the closet.

"Is this just because you want to have sex with me in this dress before we go out to dinner?" Margaret raised her leg and started pulling off her shoe. "Okay, if you make it quick."

"No, no." Kevin opened the closet, retrieved his jacket and eased himself into it. "I'm just a little preoccupied. You know, since we closed the case and all."

"Really," Margaret did a balancing act to replace her shoe, and then reached down for her coat. "Who was it?"

"Heidelman." Kevin stepped around her and helped her slip into her coat. He had waited to tell her about the outcome of the case until now, wanting to see her expression when she was told who the killer was. "He was running a protection racket for MacDonald, and became his local muscle and triggerman, cleaning up his messes."

"And I take it everyone became a mess sooner or later in MacDonald's mind?" Margaret asked archly.

Kevin replied as he walked to the door, "Yes, everyone." Suddenly, he turned to face Margaret, staring into her big, bright blue eyes as she came to the door, waiting for him to open it.

"I'm so very much in love with you, Em," he said.

"Em?" She asked, taken aback. "David calls me that."

But Kevin reached out, pinched her chin playfully, and planted a tender kiss on her lips. "I love you, Margaret."

She kissed him back, then gave him a light slap on his cheek. "You'd *better*," she laughed.

the end

THE STORY CONTINUES...

After the suspicious death of his father, Kevin Whitehouse returns to his hometown of Brandon, Vermont to attend his father's funeral. In short order, he uncovers clues pointing to the probability that his father's death was no accident. The murder investigation that ensues plunges Kevin and David into a circus of lies and deceit, as the homicide rate in this sleepy New England town begins to rise. Big-city police work clashes with small-town attitudes as the two savvy private investigators scour every nook and cranny to flush out the killer and his motives before he kills again—in *The Edge of Darkness*.

Sign up now to receive the latest news on the release date of the second novel in the "Darkness" series (www.darknessnovels.com/contact.aspx)

www.ingramcontent.com/pod-product-compliance
Lightning Source LLC
Chambersburg PA
CBHW051509170626
46811CB00002B/722